POISONED FREEBIES AT PHOEBE'S

AN IVY CREEK COZY MYSTERY

RUTH BAKER

CLEANTALES PUBLISHING

OTHER BOOKS IN THE IVY CREEK SERIES

AN IVY CREEK COZY MYSTERY

BOOK TWELVE

1

"*I* think I'll have the strawberry patch salad," Lucy said as she closed her menu and set it down on the bistro table. "I'm ready for the flavors of summer!"

She smiled at Betsy, her friend and youngest employee, who was leaning back in her chair, her face tipped up to the sunshine, and eyes closed. "Have you decided?"

Betsy straightened back up and sighed. "As much as I'd love the blueberry crepes, I'll follow your lead and get a salad." She made a face. "My mom says I need to count my calories until after the wedding."

Lucy couldn't help but chuckle. "You? You have nothing to worry about, Betsy." She sipped at her iced coffee, studying Betsy's face. "How are the wedding plans going?"

Betsy cracked a smile. "I've got my wedding cake vendor nailed down, but that's about it."

Lucy grinned. As the owner of Sweet Delights Bakery, she was pretty psyched to be designing Betsy and Joseph's

3

wedding cake. Hannah Curry, her right-hand employee, and best friend, would be baking the cake layers and helping with the decorating–both tasks were Hannah's specialty. Lucy was all about the design aspect, herself–the sketching of a concept and turning it into an edible work of art - though she was no slouch with a pastry bag, either.

The waitress appeared, and the ladies placed their order. As the server walked away, Lucy's eyes roamed the bustling sidewalk. It seemed that everyone in Ivy Creek had the same idea today—to get out into the welcome sunshine and kick off the start of summer. It was about time! Colorado winters were notoriously long and extremely cold, and spring was only marginally better.

Betsy fiddled with her straw, looking up to meet Lucy's eyes. "This is fun, Lucy. Thanks for inviting me. I know it's not very often you have a day off."

Lucy smiled graciously. "It's even more rare that both of us have a day off, together. It was nice of Aunt Tricia and Hannah to cover the bakery today."

Betsy nodded. "Has Tricia started her garden yet?"

Lucy's aunt, with whom Lucy shared a house, was famous for her bountiful vegetable gardens each year, and often won ribbons in the county fair for her prized heirloom tomatoes.

Lucy shook her head. "Actually, before I go home, I've been instructed to pick up a few flats of vegetables at Zander's Nursery. Summer squash, cucumbers, and red bell peppers. Aunt Tricia started seeds weeks ago for the rest."

Betsy sighed dreamily. "I can't wait until all this wedding hubbub is over, and Joseph and I can settle into married life… I plan to have a big vegetable garden, and lots of flowers, too."

Their food arrived, and conversation slowed as they sampled the fare. As always, Rick's Café served delicious, fresh food at a reasonable price.

Lucy had briefly dated the owner when she first moved back to Ivy Creek, after years of living in the city, working as a food blogger. The tragic death of her parents had brought her back to her hometown, and eventually back into the arms of her high school sweetheart, Taylor Baker, who was now the deputy sheriff. The decision to stay and take over her parents' bakery was one of the best choices she'd ever made, Lucy reflected, skewering a strawberry. Small town life suited her.

Betsy swallowed a bite. "You know, for a salad, this is pretty good! Speaking of food, Mom keeps insisting we have chicken and steak for the reception, but Joseph says he wants a vegetarian option. What do you think?"

Lucy patted her lips with a napkin, choosing her words carefully. "I think you and Joseph should pick what you like best. This is your big day, after all."

Betsy sighed. "Tell that to my mother. She's got a totally different vision of the whole event." She laid down her fork, reaching for her iced tea. "I just don't see the wisdom of spending thousands of dollars for one day of celebration. It would be easier if we just eloped."

Lucy was surprised. "Are you considering eloping?"

Betsy pursed her lips. "It's come up. But we're both too afraid of disappointing our families. I guess we'll just go with the flow."

The conversation drifted to other subjects as they lingered over their food, enjoying the sun warming their skin. Eventually, Betsy looked at her watch, with an exclamation of surprise.

"Wow, two o'clock already! I should be going. I'm meeting Joseph at the theater in an hour." Betsy's fiancé was the director of the Ivy Creek Playhouse. Betsy often helped him with production details.

The ladies stood, settling their tab.

"Say hello to Joseph!" Lucy called as they went their separate ways on the sidewalk. Betsy waved a hand in acknowledgement, and Lucy turned back around, covering the short distance to Zander's nursery in no time at all.

She cruised the outdoor aisles, placing Aunt Tricia's requested vegetable seedlings in her cart, and paused by a display of celosia and phlox, tempted by the bright colors. On impulse, she added a flat of each to her cart, and proceeded to checkout.

Minutes later, Lucy was walking briskly down the sidewalk again, her purchases neatly arranged in a shallow cardboard box. It was only a half a block from where she was parked. She glanced at her watch, pleased to see she had much of the afternoon left ahead of her.

I could get used to having an entire day off, she thought, window shopping as she walked down the cobblestone sidewalk. *Maybe this year I should strive for more personal time.*

Her reflection stared back at her from an empty shop window as she paused, momentarily confused by the cavernous, unlit storefront before her eyes.

Wait...what? Wasn't this Georgio's Pizza?

Lucy stepped back and looked up, feeling disoriented, her eyes searching for the store's sign.

Permanently Closed

The sad white banner hung haphazardly over the familiar red and white pizzeria logo that had been in place for decades.

Lucy was stunned, staring at the banner with her mouth gaping open, before peering into the abandoned shop where she had spent so many afternoons as a teenager. A lump formed in her throat.

Georgio's Pizza... gone. A piece of her past had disappeared.

Lucy sighed and trudged on with a heavy heart. Memories flitted through her mind in rapid-fire succession. *Sitting at the chipped formica table with a group of girlfriends, making eyes at the table full of boys huddled in the corner. Playing Pac Man and Space Invaders on the arcade machines. Flirting with Taylor, hoping he'd notice her new, fuzzy, purple sweater. The first sweet kiss between them, that had happened when he walked her home from a pizza date...*

Lucy stopped at her SUV, setting the box down on the hood and fishing out her keys. She tried to brush away the melancholy feeling. *Places were never permanent*, she told herself. She still had her memories.

As Lucy settled into the driver's seat, the box stowed safely in the back, her phone rang, startling her.

She squinted at the display. It was Hannah.

"Hey, Hannah, is everything OK?"

Hannah's voice came over the line, her tone bursting with excitement.

"Don't worry - everything's good at the bakery. But I have news... I couldn't wait till tomorrow to tell you!"

2

*L*ucy's eyebrows went up. Hannah sounded psyched. "What is it?"

"Miles is going out of town to attend a theater conference in Canada. It's a really big event, and he's combining it with a trip to visit some old college friends, so he'll be gone for two weeks."

Lucy's heart sank. *Was Hannah asking for time off?* With wedding cake season just beginning, she really needed her help.

"And...?" Lucy prompted, shutting her eyes and crossing her fingers.

"He's asked me to take care of Sampson while he's gone!" Hannah announced triumphantly.

Lucy relaxed. Sampson was Miles's newly adopted white shepherd, rescued from a dog shelter just a month before. "Oh, that's so great! It's better than boarding him. Cheaper, too."

"No kidding," Hannah agreed. "Because Sampson was in the shelter so long, Miles is afraid he'd feel abandoned if he boarded him, especially since he just recently came to live with him." She sighed happily. "I've been wanting a chance to bond with Sampson."

Lucy grinned. Hannah had such a soft spot for animals. She and Miles were a match made in heaven. Miles had been fostering abandoned greyhounds when Hannah had met him, providing the dogs a temporary home while they were matched with new "parents". And Hannah had rescued her own cat, Spooky, not too long ago, when the stray had begun hanging around the bakery.

The thought of Spooky prompted Lucy's next question.

"Are you bringing Sampson to your place?"

Hannah replied affirmatively. "Yeah, we talked about me bringing Spooky to his place, and staying there, but my place is more convenient to the bakery." Her voice took on a hopeful tone. "With any luck, the two of them will get along."

Lucy tried to think positive, but she couldn't help but wonder if it might not be that easy. "Well… it's only for two weeks. I'm sure you can make it work." She changed the subject.

"How did it go at the bakery today?"

"Just fine," Hannah replied. "Mrs. Davies came in, wanting to talk to you about her daughter's wedding cake. You'll probably see her tomorrow. How was lunch with Betsy?"

Lucy spent the next few minutes detailing her experience at Rick's, commending the food and service. Then she brought up the only bleak spot in her day.

"Did you know Georgio's Pizza closed up?" Lucy knew Hannah had spent many afternoons there, too, back in their high school days.

"What?" Hannah exclaimed, shocked. "Oh, no!" She sounded as dismayed as Lucy felt.

"I know," Lucy commiserated. "The end of an era." A car slowed down next to her, the driver eyeing Lucy's parking spot.

"I've got to get going, Hannah. That's great about Sampson! I can't wait to meet him."

"You'll love him!" Hannah replied. "He's like a giant teddy bear. OK, see you tomorrow."

They both hung up, and Lucy pulled out onto the street, thinking about Sampson and Spooky.

With any luck, the pair would both mind their manners, and not cause Hannah too much grief.

A short time later, Lucy pulled into her own driveway, admiring the rhododendron bushes on either side, in full bloom now. She gathered up her box full of seedlings and shouldered her way through the front door, kicking it shut with her heel.

Her white Persian cat, Gigi, appeared at once, twining around her ankles.

"Hello, pretty baby," Lucy crooned. "Why aren't you outside on this beautiful day?"

Gigi had her own entrance–a cat door in the kitchen. Usually, when the weather was warm, the feline would spend her days lounging on the brick patio just beyond the back door.

Gigi meowed back in response, leading the way into the kitchen in a meandering fashion, checking to make sure Lucy followed. Setting her cardboard box by the back door, Lucy could see her aunt out in the yard, a shovel in her hand as she stood in the middle of the garden.

Lucy watched her with admiration as she retrieved a cat treat for Gigi. Aunt Tricia was nearly seventy years old, but remained very active, not afraid of rolling up her sleeves to get a job done.

Lucy picked up the box of plants and opened the back door, allowing Gigi to scoot through ahead of her.

"I've got your veggies, Auntie!" she called out, walking across the yard to join her. Gigi scampered on ahead, leaping onto the freshly turned soil and making a show of crouching in a predatory pose, eyes slitted, tail swishing.

"Get out of there, Gigi!" Aunt Tricia scolded, clapping her hands.

Ears flattened, Gigi bolted, running for the sanctuary of a nearby shrubbery. She sulked beneath the low branches.

Aunt Tricia turned to inspect the box Lucy held with an approving eye. "Very healthy. I'll get these in the ground today. Before you know it, we'll be having fresh vegetables every night."

She eyed the flowers in the box with one eyebrow raised. "I knew you wouldn't be able to get in and out of Zander's without buying more flowers."

Lucy grinned sheepishly. She'd inherited her mother's love for pretty flowers, though, sad to say, she hadn't inherited her green thumb. Aunt Tricia was constantly rescuing Lucy's flowers, bringing them back from death's door.

"I thought they'd look pretty in the pots out front," Lucy ventured. "And they're such vibrant and healthy plants."

"So far…" Aunt Tricia teased her, and Lucy chuckled.

She heard the sudden chime of her cell phone through the open kitchen window and set down the box of plants.

"That's my phone," she called over her shoulder, hurrying for the door.

By the time she'd fished her phone out of her purse, it had stopped ringing. She looked at the display. *It was Taylor*; she realized with a smile.

She'd originally hoped they could spend today together, but as deputy sheriff of Ivy Creek, Taylor's responsibilities were enormous. He and Lucy didn't often get to spend an entire day together. The bakery was one of Taylor's daily stops, however, and he was a regular guest for dinner at Lucy and Aunt Tricia's house.

She quickly dialed his cell number, and soon his welcome voice came over the line.

"How was your day, sweetheart? Did you remember to relax?"

Lucy grinned at his teasing tone. She did like to stay busy, always involved in some project. "I did," she countered. "And Betsy and I had a very nice lunch at Rick's Café."

"Oh, that's good to hear. Wedding plans going well?"

Lucy wandered through the house as she filled him in, relaying how Betsy's mother had some strong opinions.

"Gosh, that must be hard," she concluded. "Trying to keep true to your own vision but feeling the pressure of someone else's wishes."

"Maybe they should elope," Taylor replied, unknowingly echoing Betsy's words.

Lucy was about to comment when she heard someone in the background calling Taylor's name. She knew what that meant.

Sure enough, she heard his muffled reply to another before he addressed her again. "Sorry, Luce, I've got to go. But I have a surprise for you."

His words made her smile. "You do? What is it?"

Taylor chuckled. "Well, if I told you, it wouldn't be a surprise, now, would it?"

Lucy giggled. "OK. How long do I have to wait?"

"Not long," he assured her. "I'll stop by the bakery with it tomorrow. I think you'll like it."

They said their goodbyes, and Lucy hung up the phone, filled with anticipation.

What could it be?

---

3

*L*ucy, Hannah, Betsy, and Aunt Tricia sat at the front table near the bakery window, having their weekly *pow wow*. It was a time-honored tradition, to trade ideas back and forth on the coming seasons and trends, and brainstorm what new products might be successful.

They had just finished discussing the addition of quiche slices, prepackaged and ready to go for their faithful lunch crowd, when Lucy observed a young man on the sidewalk walking by with a handful of flyers. He slipped one under their door, as the bakery sign still read 'closed'.

Curious, Lucy stood and walked to the entrance, stooping to retrieve the colorful advertisement.

Her eyes scanned the page as she returned to the table.

"Hey, guys, look at this!" She held it up for the others to see.

Phoebe's Bridal Shop – Grand Opening!

"Ooh..." Betsy's eyes sparkled with interest. "Right here in Ivy Creek, and just for the ladies!" She clapped her hands. "How perfect!"

"I wonder what Crane's Formal Wear thinks about this," Aunt Tricia commented, referring to the long-established business in town, which concentrated mostly on renting tuxes and prom gowns to Ivy Creek's citizens.

Betsy made a face. "I stopped in to check out their wedding gowns. No more than four styles, and none were modern at all."

Hannah commented diplomatically, "But they have a great selection of tuxes for the men." She looked over at Lucy with a grin. "And probably half the women of Ivy Creek bought their prom gown there, over the years! I know *I* did."

Lucy chuckled. "Me, too. Unless you wanted to travel to the city, Crane's is where you went."

Betsy declared. "Well, times are changing, and I'm glad Ivy Creek is changing with them." She peered more closely at the fine print. "It says they'll be having a fashion show, with a runway and catered refreshments." She glanced up at Lucy. "Are we providing refreshments?"

Lucy shook her head. "Must not be. I haven't received a request for a quote."

Hannah joked, "Not yet..."

Lucy smiled, but privately she hoped it wasn't going to be a last-minute surprise. Just the number of emails and phone calls about wedding and graduation cakes so far had her thinking this summer would be really busy at Sweet Delights.

Aunt Tricia asked, "Where is it going to be? On Main Street?"

Betsy traced the type with one finger, nodding her head. "It says sixteen hundred Main Street." She tilted her head inquisitively. "Where is that, exactly? Near Zander's?"

Lucy and Hannah spoke at the same time.

"That's Georgio's Pizza's location!"

Lucy's eyes widened. "Wow, they didn't waste any time. Georgio's just closed down."

Aunt Tricia nodded. "Prime real estate, there. I bet they'll do well."

Betsy looked around at the other ladies. "Let's all go together!" Her eyes pleaded with them. "It will be fun!"

Hannah groaned in mock despair, and Lucy elbowed her. "We could do that. Close the bakery early that day."

Aunt Tricia looked at Betsy over the top of her spectacles. "Won't your mother feel left out, dear?"

Betsy rolled her eyes. "She wouldn't go, anyway. She's been pushing me to have her old wedding dress altered, but I'm not crazy about the style. I just haven't had the heart to outright refuse… yet…"

Hannah raised one eyebrow. "Well, buying a new gown should certainly get the message across." She glanced around at the other ladies, then met Betsy's eyes. "I was just teasing you, Betsy. I'm not into all that girly stuff myself, but I know this is a big deal for you. Of course, I'll go."

"Yay!" Betsy cheered, as the other women nodded their agreement. "I'm really looking forward to it." She pointed to one corner of the flyer. "Look here, it says there will be a surprise special guest. I wonder who that will be?"

Lucy shook her head and stood up. It was time to open the shop. "Guess we'll find out when we get there."

Aunt Tricia smirked, pushing her chair back in. "Oh, this town's no good at secrets. I'm sure we'll find out well before then."

Lucy walked to the blackboard they advertised their daily specials on, reaching for a piece of chalk. "Speaking of surprises, Taylor said he's bringing me a surprise today."

Betsy's eyes widened. "What do you think it is? An engagement ring?"

Lucy's hand stopped in mid-scrawl. She turned to look back, panic in her eyes.

"Oh, my…" She hadn't considered that possibility and wasn't quite sure how she felt about it.

Hannah laughed. "He has more class than that, Lucy. He's not going to ask you to marry him in front of all of us, here at the bakery, as he stops in for his coffee!"

Lucy smiled at the mental image. *That was probably true.*

Aunt Tricia sniffed. "As long as the two of you have been dating, some might say it's high time you tied the knot."

Lucy kept writing on the chalkboard, but she couldn't help grinning at Aunt Tricia's words. Though she dearly loved her aunt, if she'd had her way, Lucy and Taylor would have been married for years by now, with several children already.

Lucy knew eventually she'd like to get married and start a family, but she was very much enjoying her life, just the way it was right now. The bakery was doing great, and she was surrounded by good friends, and free to make plans on a whim. She didn't want all that to change, just yet.

The first customer arrived, and a steady stream of regulars filtered in soon after. Lucy and Hannah retreated to the back room, which housed their kitchen and decorating space, while Aunt Tricia and Betsy kept up with the sales.

As Lucy returned to the front room sporadically, replenishing empty pastry trays, her ears picked up snippets of conversation revolving around the new bridal shop in town. Everyone seemed excited, and all had their own theories about the special guest.

"I wonder if it could be the governor's wife?" One woman ventured to her friend, sitting at a small table near the pastry case. "Their daughter, Julia, is planning a wedding."

Another woman stood at the counter, chatting with Aunt Tricia. "I bet Phoebe's special guest will be a local musician from the area. Maybe Anna Jones, who does that classical guitar stuff. She's pretty popular."

The speculation went on through the morning. *The town was certainly buzzing about the new shop,* Lucy reflected. *Phoebe's grand opening would no doubt be well-attended.*

The crowd had finally thinned down as the clock hit ten-thirty. In another hour, their lunch rush would begin, and Taylor had not yet shown up.

Lucy tried to keep her mind on the recipe she was following, but her attention kept wavering. Normally, she liked surprises, but now she found herself slightly anxious. *What if it was something entirely unexpected, like tickets for a romantic getaway?*

She knew Taylor was aware she wanted them to spend more time together, as they'd just discussed that topic last

Christmas. But right now would not be a good time to get away. Spring was one of her busiest seasons.

Lucy added flour to her batter, turning the mixer on. *Come to think of it, summer was pretty busy, too. And fall. Not so much winter... well, except for Christmas. And Valentine's Day, of course.* Her head began to swim. If Taylor wanted them to take a trip together, Lucy didn't know when the best time would be. Her forehead creased as she tried to imagine a conversation about that.

"What's going on over there?" Hannah called out in a teasing tone. "You look like that cake batter is giving you grief."

Lucy looked up, startled, then grinned sheepishly. "I'm just trying to guess what Taylor's surprise will be," she admitted. "I'm making myself nervous about it."

Hannah's eyes traveled to the archway separating the kitchen from the front space.

"Well, I think you're about to find out," she commented, her eyes crinkling with amusement.

Lucy quickly turned in that direction. Taylor was leaned up against the doorjamb, arms folded, with a cocky grin on his face.

"Are you ready? You're going to love this, I promise."

4

*L*ucy couldn't help but smile at the expression on Taylor's face. He looked so eager, like a little boy with a secret. She shut off the mixer and wiped her hands on a towel.

"I sure am!" she replied enthusiastically. "Lead the way."

Taylor instructed her, "Close your eyes." He held her arm, and Lucy complied, allowing him to lead her out to the front room.

She heard Betsy giggle as Taylor positioned her, finally saying, "OK. You can look now."

Lucy opened up her eyes, not sure of what to expect. The large object was directly in front of her, and she gasped, covering her mouth with her hand.

It was the jukebox from Georgio's Pizza.

"I can't believe it!" she crowed with delight, moving to stand before it. She turned her head to regard Taylor, who stood with his arms folded, enjoying her obvious pleasure.

"I didn't even know if you were aware they'd closed," she said, grinning. "I just found out, myself."

"That is just too cool," Hannah said admiringly. "Nice job, Taylor."

Lucy ran her hands over the familiar structure. "This is just perfect," she declared, her eyes shining. She turned and looped her arms around Taylor's waist, giving him a hug. "It's like we're preserving a bit of our past."

"But where are we going to put it?" Aunt Tricia asked, ever practical.

Taylor considered the space, outlining the possibilities. "Maybe over by the honey display? So it will be out of the way, but the customers will still notice it."

"Sounds great," Lucy agreed. She turned to the machine again, flipping through the song list. "Wow, they've got some of our golden oldies on here, still."

She turned to Hannah with a grin. "I remember you used to love that song by The Fray. Do you remember?"

Hannah nodded, her eyes sparkling with the memory. "How to Save a Life. I haven't heard it in forever. Is it on there, still?"

"Sure is!"

Betsy tilted her head. "I don't think I've ever heard that one."

"Before your time, I guess," Lucy told her, as Taylor used the hand truck to wheel the jukebox across the room. He straightened it square to the wall and plugged it in.

"You're in for a treat," Hannah told Betsy, fishing into her pocket for a dollar bill. She punched in the corresponding number, and the introductory notes of the song washed over them.

Betsy closed her eyes dreamily and listened for a minute. "It's pretty, but sad," she concluded.

"As all great songs are," Hannah informed her.

Taylor glanced at the clock. "Well, I'd love to stay and listen, but I've got to get back."

Lucy offered, "Let me get you a coffee and pastry. That was such a nice gesture, Taylor, and a lovely surprise! Thank you."

He looked pleased with himself, accepting the coffee and bakery bag she passed to him.

"I'll call you tonight," he said to Lucy, waving at the others and heading for the door.

Aunt Tricia waited until the final notes of the song faded away before she spoke.

"OK, ladies, the lunch rush is about to begin. Let's keep the music low."

Hannah complied, turning down the volume, and joining Lucy behind the counter.

"Wow, that was some surprise! I'm so glad Taylor rescued a piece of our past."

Lucy grinned, agreeing. It had been such an unexpected gesture and took some of the sting away from losing her childhood hangout. *He was a sweet, sweet man*, she reflected. She counted herself lucky.

Aunt Tricia set up a crockpot for their soup of the day, and Betsy made a few ready-to-go sandwiches as the jukebox played softly in the background.

The lunch regulars began to drift in, all of them exclaiming over the new addition to the bakery. The talk centered on Georgio's Pizza, and everyone's memories of the iconic Ivy Creek business, with several of the customers sharing their own experiences there.

Everyone had heard of the new bridal shop opening up, but no one had any idea who the special guest would be… until Mrs. White stopped by in the early afternoon.

Mrs. White was a regular customer, notorious for her large orders, often buying out their stock on particular items in one fell swoop. She had a big family and adored supplying them with fresh-baked treats at least three times a week.

She was also the most prolific gossip in Ivy Creek, so it came as no surprise to Lucy when she burst into the bakery with an announcement.

"Ladies, have you heard? Vanna Verity will attend the grand opening of the new bridal shop!"

"Vanna Verity?" Lucy echoed, brows raised. "Impressive!"

Hannah poked her head out from the kitchen. "Did you say Vanna Verity? Is she bringing that hot fiancé of hers?"

Betsy shook her head, puzzled. "Am I the only one here who doesn't know who Vanna Verity is?"

Aunt Tricia explained. "She's an Ivy Creek native who had a talk show for almost a decade, but it's been off the air for at least five years now."

"Oh, OK," Betsy nodded. "I think maybe I remember my mom watching her show. How cool is that? I'll get to meet an actual celebrity!"

"That's right!" Mrs. White said, nodding approvingly. "Here in Ivy Creek, we are proud to claim her as one of our own. I, for one, will be asking for her autograph."

"Are you going to the bridal show, Mrs. White?" Aunt Tricia asked. "Just wondering, as your oldest daughter is only sixteen, isn't she?"

Lucy hid a grin as Mrs. White clucked her tongue. "You can't start planning a wedding too soon, Tricia, as you know. It will be good just to see what this Phoebe person will have to offer."

Turning away, she leaned over the pastry case, studying the choices.

"Could I have two dozen of those turtle brownies, please? And four blueberry turnovers."

Glancing back up, her eyes connected with Lucy's. "I hear the grand opening will be a catered event. Please tell me you'll be serving some of those delicious cream puffs."

Lucy was taken aback. "I… ah, the event won't be catered by Sweet Delights."

Mrs. White looked shocked. "No? Well, who on earth will be providing refreshments, then?"

Lucy shrugged. "I guess we'll have to wait and see."

Personally, she was a bit curious. The more she heard about the event, the more intrigued she became. Phoebe was certainly pulling out all the stops to make an impression on the people of Ivy Creek.

What other surprises might be in store?

---

5

*L*ucy yawned, stretching her arms overhead and waking Gigi, who was snuggled next to her pillow. The feline pinned her with a censuring look, flattening her ears with disapproval before hopping down from the bed.

Lucy peered at the clock and reluctantly followed suit. Moments later, she emerged from the bathroom, tightening the belt of her robe, and following the scent of coffee from the kitchen.

Halfway down the hall, she heard a cry of dismay. "No!"

It was Aunt Tricia!

"Auntie? What is it?" Lucy raced down the hall, heart pounding, and skidded to a halt on the kitchen threshold.

Her aunt stood at the kitchen window, looking out at the backyard in the early morning light, with her fist held to her mouth in dismay.

Lucy joined her, her eyes scanning the yard to see what was amiss.

Oh no! The vegetable garden lay in ruins, stalks chomped off and plants uprooted. The entire garden was a mess, the soil tromped upon by scavenging wildlife.

"Maybe it's not as bad as it looks," Lucy mumbled, trading her slippers for garden boots at the door. "I'll go take a look."

She opened the door and stepped outside, with Aunt Tricia following as far as the edge of the brick patio. The older woman stood with her arms crossed, her face pinched with displeasure as she watched Lucy examine the plants.

"Did they destroy everything? Was it rabbits, do you think?"

Lucy glumly fingered the battered stalks, devoid of all leaves. Her eyes scanned the upturned soil, looking for clues.

Aha! Hoof prints.

"It was deer," she reported. "And, yes, Auntie, I'm afraid they chewed everything... except for this..." Lucy peered at the single unmolested plant, searching for the tag her aunt always stuck in the soil. "They left the summer squash alone," she announced, hoping to cheer her.

Aunt Tricia looked disgusted. "But they ate my tomato plants! And all my carrots, my lettuce, and spinach..."

Lucy spotted a small pile of droppings nearby and amended her original answer. "The deer had help. It looks like the rabbits joined them for a party."

Aunt Tricia snorted, turning on her heel and walking back inside in a bad temper.

Lucy straightened up, wondering how to solve the problem. She and her aunt were committed to gardening organically. What could be done to prevent the return of the deer and rabbits?

Pondering this, she walked back inside, sorely needing a jolt of caffeine.

Hopefully, the rest of the day would prove less challenging.

———

LUCY ARRIVED at the bakery at seven-thirty sharp, surprised to find the kitchen still unlit, and the ovens cold. Usually, Hannah arrived by six-thirty or seven to begin baking the morning's pastries. She switched the ovens on and meandered out front to start some coffee, hoping that everything was OK.

Fifteen minutes later, as she was reviewing yesterday's sales receipts, she heard the back entrance open and close. Moments later, a bedraggled-looking Hannah trudged through the kitchen archway, yawning widely. She waved mutely at Lucy, pouring herself a cup of coffee.

Lucy waited until her friend had taken a sip, seeming to savor the strong brew.

"Ah… is everything alright?" Lucy asked cautiously. "Did you not sleep well?"

Hannah crossed the room and slumped into the chair across from her. Her hair was mussed, her eyes bloodshot, and her shirt badly wrinkled.

"No sleep," she confessed. "Not a wink. Playing referee all night long." She buried her nose in her coffee cup, closing her eyes.

Lucy frowned. "Referee? Oh…" The light dawned in her eyes. "You're talking about Sampson. You picked him up yesterday?"

Hannah nodded, setting her cup down and running a hand over her face wearily.

"Turns out Sampson and Spooky don't like each other." She held up a finger. "Correction. Sampson thinks Spooky looks delicious. Spooky, understandably, hates Sampson."

"Oh, no!" Lucy was horrified. "Did he try to–"

"Yep." Hannah nodded, her green eyes troubled. "Several times. I finally had to shut him in the laundry room."

"Isn't Spooky's litter box in there?" Lucy asked, brows raised.

Hannah sighed. "Not anymore. Now her bathroom is in *my* bathroom."

Lucy made a sympathetic noise. Hannah sighed, rolling her neck to work out the kinks.

"And then he barked all night long. I mean–*all night long*! The boy's got some serious vocal chords."

She looked at Lucy hopefully. "Do you have any advice on getting him to calm down? I mean, I can't do this for two whole weeks."

Lucy thought for a moment. "Where is he now?"

Hannah waved a hand. "He's got the run of the house. Spooky just wanted to get outside this morning. Can't say I blame her. But I don't like for her to go out at night."

"How about a baby gate?" Lucy suggested. "Put it at the end of the hallway, so Sampson has the kitchen and living room, and then Spooky will have your bedroom and the laundry room."

Hannah sat up straighter, considering the idea. "That could work…" she mused. Her eyes met Lucy's speculatively. "Do you know anyone who has a baby gate they're not using?"

Lucy pursed her lips, thinking. "I think Aunt Tricia's friend, Connie, has one. And she only uses hers when her granddaughter is over. She'd probably lend it to you."

Hannah drew a weary breath, nodding her head. "I'll ask Tricia when she gets in. Where is she, anyway? Does she have today off?"

Lucy shook her head. "Her garden was destroyed by rabbits and deer overnight. When I left the house, she was still looking up natural deterrents on the web."

Hannah looked crushed. "Destroyed? Does that mean I won't be getting any free veggies this year?"

Lucy chuckled. "Well, you can have all the summer squash you want. Apparently, the wildlife around here is picky. Not a leaf was harmed on the crookneck squash."

Hannah made a face. "Can't say I blame them."

The bell jangled, and Betsy came through the door, calling out a cheery hello. She took one look at Hannah and stopped in her tracks. "What happened to you?"

Hannah's mouth twisted with dry humor. "Sampson is not minding his manners."

"Oh, no…" Betsy's eyes were sympathetic. "He and Spooky?"

Hannah nodded. "Fighting like cats and dogs."

Betsy stifled a chuckle, walking to the counter and helping herself to a cup of coffee.

As she stirred a shot of hazelnut syrup into her drink, the bakery telephone rang. She looked to Lucy for direction, seeing that it was nearly an hour before they opened.

"Shall I?"

Lucy nodded, and Betsy picked up the receiver. "Thank you for calling Sweet Delights Bakery. This is Betsy. How may I help you?"

She listened for a moment, then said, "Just one minute, please. Who shall I say is calling?"

Her eyes widened. She turned to Lucy, covering the mouthpiece.

"It's Jackson Louis. The owner of Classic Fare Catering."

---

6

*L*ucy rose and walked to the counter, taking the receiver. *What could this be about?*

"Hello, Mr. Louis. This is Lucy Hale. How can I help you?"

The man's voice boomed through the receiver, and Lucy winced, holding it away from her ear.

"Good morning, Ms. Hale. I trust you've heard about Phoebe's Bridal Shop's grand opening event?"

Lucy replied affirmatively, turning her head as the bakery door opened and Aunt Tricia came in. "Yes, I have. We're planning to attend."

Mr. Louis sounded pleased. "That's wonderful. It's high time we made each other's acquaintance. I'm calling to ask a favor. Classic Fare has been hired to cater the event, but I've run into a snag. I hope that you–as an expert in desserts–could give me some advice."

Curiosity piqued, Lucy asked, "I'd be happy to do whatever I can, Mr. Louis. What exactly are you needing?"

Aunt Tricia made herself a latte and moved to Lucy's side, making no pretense as she leaned in to overhear the conversation.

"Well, as I'm sure you've heard, Vanna Verity will be present, along with her entourage. I've been contacted by the mayor, as he thinks this will be a very good publicity event for our town. Vanna Verity is practically a household name. There will be a full write-up in The Ivy Creek Ledger."

Lucy raised her brows. *A very good publicity opportunity for Classic Fare,* she thought.

"I see," she murmured, still wondering what exactly Mr. Louis needed.

"The problem arose when a Ms. Ritner–who I assume is Ms. Verity's personal assistant–contacted me with a list of her employer's dietary preferences. According to the list, Ms. Verity avoids wheat products, refined sugar, and is strictly vegan. To be honest, that throws a wrench in our plans. We had intended to serve petit fours, and I told the mayor we would make a special star-shaped petit four specifically for Vanna. He thought it would be a nice welcoming gesture to our returning "star", you see?"

Lucy's forehead wrinkled. "If I'm understanding you, you're looking for a petit four recipe that is vegan, gluten-free, and sugar free. Is that correct?"

A pause, then Mr. Louis replied. "Is there such a thing in existence?"

Lucy was silent for a moment, considering. "I think it can be done. You could use date paste as a binder instead of eggs, and it's sweet, as well. Almond flour instead of wheat. And if you combine sugar-free white chocolate chips with coconut milk, that could work for the glaze."

"Fantastic!" Mr. Louis boomed, and Lucy pulled the receiver away from her ear. "Would you be so kind as to write up a recipe and email it over? I would be forever in your debt."

Lucy agreed, adding, "No problem at all. But please be aware, while vegan, sugar-free, and gluten-free desserts may be healthier, they oftentimes fail to please the palate the way regular desserts do… it's really a matter of what you're used to. So, you may want to serve regular petit fours to the rest of the patrons, and just use the modified recipe for the star-shaped cake."

"Hmm. Yes, I see your point." With a final expression of gratitude, Mr. Louis supplied his email address, and Lucy told him she'd send him a recipe later that day. She hung up the phone to see Aunt Tricia, Hannah, and Betsy waiting expectantly.

She quickly filled them in on the request, and Hannah burst out laughing.

"I guess it's a good thing Classic Fare is dealing with that, and not us."

Privately, Lucy agreed. It sounded like Vanna Verity may be hard to please.

The ladies went about the business of opening up the shop, and soon the phone began to ring with custom orders coming in. Several customers stopped by to discuss tiered cake designs with Lucy, as both graduation season and wedding season were right around the corner. The task of sketching out the visions her customers described brought Lucy pleasure, and the day went by quickly.

By late afternoon, things had slowed down considerably. Lucy sent out the promised email to Classic Fare before conferring with Hannah over the ingredients they would need for the rest of the week. Although Lucy tended to buy her flour and sugar from suppliers who delivered the product to her door, she liked using local businesses for the rest of her needs.

Aunt Tricia would be closing that afternoon, so Lucy left a little early to stop by Bing's Grocery, her favorite local supplier. She browsed through the baking aisle, checking off her list and grabbing up a few items that were on sale. Soon, she was standing in line at the checkout counter, her mind wandering as she half-tuned in to the chatter of the ladies behind her.

"I heard that Vanna Verity will be at Phoebe's Bridal Shop's grand opening."

Her companion chuckled. "No kidding–they've hung a huge banner at the edge of town already, welcoming her back as the Hometown Queen."

The first woman snickered. "More like Hometown Has-Been! I don't think she's done a thing since she was replaced as the host of that talk show… what was it called?"

Her friend supplied the title, "*Vanna's View*. They changed it though, to *Coffee with Kim*."

The line moved forward a bit, and Lucy began loading her items on the conveyor belt. The conversation behind her continued, and she tried to ignore it.

"She must be pretty hard up for attention to come to the opening of a small shop in an even smaller town. I suppose The Ivy Creek Ledger will be there, but still…"

RUTH BAKER

"Isn't she engaged to that actor? What's his name? You know, with the hipster beard. Maybe they're actually shopping for a wedding gown. She *is* from here, after all."

The other woman scoffed. "I bet it's all a publicity stunt. Just trying to jumpstart her career again with some feel-good story about her returning to her small-town roots."

Lucy turned her attention to greeting the cashier, more than willing to tune out the negativity behind her.

When did the people of Ivy Creek get so cynical?

She hoped at least some of the residents would give Vanna a warm welcome when she arrived in town.

Lucy wheeled her cart out to the parking lot and had just begun loading her SUV when her cell phone rang. She glanced down at the display. *Aunt Tricia.*

"Hello, Auntie. Is everything OK there?"

Aunt Tricia replied, "Oh, yes, I was just hoping to catch you before you checked out. Am I too late?"

Lucy assured her, "I haven't left yet. At least, not the parking lot. I'll be happy to go back in and pick up whatever you need."

"Oh, good. Thank you, dear," Aunt Tricia replied. Her next words startled Lucy.

"I need three bottles of ground cayenne pepper, please. I'll explain later."

36

7

*H*annah looked mystified as Lucy related the tale. It was early the following day, and she and Lucy were making the morning's muffins.

"Cayenne pepper? What did she need that much pepper for?"

Lucy chuckled as she stirred chopped cranberries and grated orange peel into the batter.

"Apparently, it's all over the internet–if you sprinkle red pepper on your garden, the deer and rabbits will leave the plants alone."

Hannah frowned. "But won't the rain wash it away?" She glanced pointedly at the small window above the industrial sink. The rain was coming down in sheets.

Lucy nodded, humor sparkling in her eyes. "Yeah… Auntie wasn't too happy when she woke up and looked out the window. But she has today off, and it's supposed to stop raining by early afternoon. And the good news is, she still has one jar of pepper left."

Hannah finished lining the muffin tins and began scooping out the batter. "Gee whiz, if you have to reapply the pepper every time it rains, that's going to be an expensive pest deterrent."

Lucy sprinkled coarse sugar over the tops of the muffins, garnishing them with a few berries, before sliding the trays into the oven.

"I think the point is, once the rabbits and deer get a mouthful of hot pepper, they learn to stay away from the plants."

Hannah nodded. "Oh, I get it. So, there's still hope for the garden, right?"

Lucy set the timer, answering over her shoulder. "Aunt Tricia stopped on her way home yesterday and bought a few more plants. We were busy planting and peppering them until dark last evening."

"Fingers crossed, the pepper trick works!" Hannah said. "I'm already daydreaming about fresh tomato sandwiches."

The ladies heard the bell jangle out front. A moment later Betsy called out a hello, appearing in the archway, shaking off her umbrella.

"This kind of weather makes me want to curl up with a cup of tea, a cat, and a good book," she declared. She turned to Hannah. "Speaking of cats, how are Sampson and Spooky?"

Hannah gave a thumbs up. "I put up the baby gate last night and so far, Sampson is staying on his side of it. I was a little nervous, but it was still in place when I got up this morning."

Betsy smiled. "Yay! Spooky must be relieved." She sighed, folding her umbrella. "I wish my problems were that easy to solve."

"What's wrong?" Lucy asked. "Is it about the wedding plans?"

Betsy nodded, her cheerful countenance disappearing. "My mother has taken over the planning of the wedding. She's already promised my cousin that he and his band will be the musical entertainment, even though Joseph and I agreed on a D.J."

"Uh-oh…" Hannah raised her brows.

Betsy continued, her mouth set grimly. "And now she's asked me to choose between two of her florist picks. I'm quite capable of choosing my own florist… thank you very much!"

"Did you say that?" Lucy asked.

Betsy grumbled, "Of course not. She's my mother, after all."

"But it's *your* wedding," Hannah protested. "She's already had her own wedding."

"I reminded her of that," Betsy replied. "You know what she said?"

"What?" Hannah and Lucy asked simultaneously.

"That she didn't get to plan her wedding either—just went with everything my grandmother wanted."

Lucy hid a grin as Hannah responded cheekily. "Well, I guess you'll have to wait until your future daughter gets married to plan a wedding, Betsy…"

Betsy regarded her with a frown. "Ha-ha. Not funny."

"Talk to Joseph about it," Lucy advised. "Maybe the two of you can figure something out."

———

THE MORNING WAS SLOWER than usual, as most folks seemed to be avoiding the rain. By the time one o'clock hit, the sun came out, and customers began to trickle in. Hannah had kept up with the baking easily and took a short break to go home and check on Sampson and Spooky, while Lucy and Betsy worked the front counter.

Lucy was wiping down the café tables when she noticed a stranger approaching the bakery. The woman looked to be in her late thirties, with black ringlets cascading down from a fashionable bun. She was wearing a powder blue lightweight trench coat, and she glanced up at the sky before opening the bakery door.

"Hello," she greeted Lucy with a smile. Her eyes were light blue, a striking contrast to her dark hair, and she seemed to be in a merry mood. She noticed Betsy behind the counter and offered a friendly wave.

"Good afternoon," Lucy said warmly. "Welcome to Sweet Delights."

"Thank you," she replied. "I'm new to town and I heard this is the best stop for an afternoon pick me up."

She came forward, offering her hand. "I'm Phoebe Pierce. I have a new business on Main Street, set to open on the fifteenth. Phoebe's Bridal Shop."

Lucy grinned. "Glad to meet you, Phoebe! I'm Lucy Hale. This is my bakery."

The women shook hands and Lucy continued, indicating Betsy. "We're all very excited about your grand opening weekend! That's Betsy Henderson. She's planning her wedding, so your shop is of particular interest to her."

"Hi, Betsy," Phoebe smiled. "How exciting for you! I hope you'll like the show. We'll have fashion models showcasing the gowns and a catalogue of vendors that might be helpful to you."

"I can't wait!" Betsy said, her eyes shining.

Phoebe turned to admire the display in the front window. An elaborate 4-tier wedding cake, with separator plates between each tier stuffed with silk flowers, gave the appearance of cake layers floating on flower layers.

"Is this your work?" Phoebe exclaimed. "It's so lovely!"

Lucy was quick to answer. "Actually, that's a collaborative effort between myself and my employee, Hannah Curry. She's a very talented baker and decorator."

Betsy added, "She'll be back in a few minutes. Can I get you a coffee, Ms. Pierce?"

Phoebe smiled, "Call me Phoebe, please." She perused the menu. "I'd love a snickerdoodle latte, thank you."

As Betsy prepared Phoebe's drink, Lucy showed her the local vendor stations set up around the front room. "…and this one is honey products from Bee Natural Farm, not far from town," she concluded.

Phoebe picked up a candle and sniffed at it, her face wreathed in smiles. "How lovely! I'm intrigued by beekeeping. I'd like to pay them a visit sometime."

"Oh, they'd love that. They welcome visitors," Lucy assured her.

Betsy crossed the room to hand Phoebe her coffee, just as the bell rang, letting in another customer. She hurried off to assist the man.

Phoebe sipped the latte, closing her eyes in appreciation. "Delicious." She eyed Lucy speculatively over the rim of the cup. "Would you be interested in collaborating with my shop at some point in the future? I have a notion of offering a package deal. All-inclusive–flowers, wedding cake, and wedding gown."

Lucy slowly nodded, finding the idea appealing. "It sounds good. My designs are priced by complexity, as well as servings, though."

Phoebe nodded. "Not a problem. You could give me, say, four design examples, at different prices per serving. Then the customer could choose based on their budget."

Lucy liked the sound of that. She smiled at the other woman. "Sounds like this isn't your first rodeo," she joked. "How long have you been in the wedding gown business?"

Phoebe rotated her coffee cup in her palms before answering. "Eleven years." Lucy thought she would elaborate, but she didn't.

"And where are you from, Phoebe?" she asked, genuinely curious.

Phoebe hesitated, looking away, before flashing Lucy a smile. "Oh, here and there," she answered lightly, before looking at her watch. "I need to get going. I was planning to pop into the florist's shop today, too. It was really nice to meet you, Lucy."

She walked to the door, calling out a goodbye to Betsy. "Nice to meet you! I'll be watching for you on the fifteenth."

She exited the shop; the bell jangling behind her.

Lucy stared after her, curiously. As friendly as Phoebe was, she sure seemed to clam up in a hurry.

Why was she so evasive? she wondered, then shook her head, scolding herself for making a mystery out of nothing.

She was probably just running late, as she'd said. No mystery there.

---

*a*unt Tricia was in the backyard when Lucy got home, sitting at the patio table, involved in a peculiar task.

Lucy approached, brow furrowed. She indicated the pile of Irish Spring soap chunks that lay before her aunt, an increasing pile as the woman deftly cut more green and white striped bars with a paring knife.

"Um… what's up?" She was almost afraid to ask.

Aunt Tricia looked up from her task. "I'm not putting all my eggs in one basket, that's what." She continued to cut one-inch cubes.

Lucy frowned, not understanding. "What do you mean?"

Aunt Tricia finished the last bar and set down her knife. "Chloe Barnes was out in her yard weeding her impatiens, so I stopped by to ask her advice about repelling deer and rabbits."

The older woman rose from the table, retrieving a pile of sharpened sticks from the edge of the patio.

"She said, when she used red pepper on her sunflowers, it brought even more deer around." She looked at Lucy, her eyes magnified by the lenses of her glasses.

"It could be that they like a little spice on their food."

Lucy burst out laughing. "But red pepper? I doubt it, Auntie. It's not like salt."

Aunt Tricia shrugged. "Since I just spent more money on vegetable flats, I don't want to risk it. Anyway, Chloe said to place skewers with soap chunks all around the garden, and that will keep the deer away. Rabbits, too. I guess wildlife doesn't like the smell of soap."

Lucy ventured, "Ah… Chloe doesn't have a vegetable garden, though, Auntie. How do you know it will work?"

Her aunt looked slightly exasperated. "Obviously, I don't. Not yet anyway. But it's worth a small purchase of soap if it might save me from buying more vegetable flats."

Lucy wasn't sure she agreed with her aunt's logic. Between the red pepper flakes and the soap, the cost of protecting the garden was going up.

Her aunt thrust a handful of sticks at her. "The sooner you help me get these done, the sooner we can sit down to dinner."

Lucy sighed, giving in. "OK," she agreed.

The ladies began at separate edges of the garden, working clockwise, skewering soap shards on sticks and hammering them into the ground.

Almost done with the task, Lucy had just finished filling her aunt in on the visit from Phoebe Pierce when they heard a car pull into the driveway, followed by a loud, booming bark.

"What in the world?" Aunt Tricia exclaimed, turning toward the sound. "Who could that be?"

Lucy had a hunch, she knew. About a minute later, Hannah's voice could be heard, using a scolding tone. "Sampson, stop that! Flowers are not for eating!"

"We're in the back, Hannah!" Lucy called, hammering the last stake in.

A moment later, her friend appeared, with a large white shepherd straining at his leash.

"Hey, Lucy! Hi, Tricia! I hope I'm not interrupting your... whatever that is you're doing..."

Perplexed, Hannah stared at the vegetable garden, surrounded by an army of sharpened sticks adorned with soap cubes. Sampson pulled her inexorably toward them, his snout raised, sniffing the air and sneezing.

"It's a pest repellant," Aunt Tricia informed her.

Hannah raised her eyebrows. "Are the deer supposed to eat the soap instead of the plants? Because I don't think that's going to work."

Lucy giggled. "No, silly. The plan is the strong scent of the soap will repel them. That's what our neighbor told Auntie, anyway."

She came forward then, stretching out a hand for Sampson to sniff. "Hello, there, Sampson. I've been wanting to meet you."

Lucy scratched his head, and Sampson swiped a tongue at her, grinning in the way that dogs do.

"How did the baby gate work today?" Lucy inquired. When Hannah had returned from lunch that afternoon, she'd reported it was holding up… so far.

Hannah shook her head, a disgusted expression on her face. "Apparently, Sampson was just biding his time. I came home to total chaos. The baby gate was down and Spooky was hiding under the bed. He must have given her a good chase first, because a lamp was knocked over, and my potted Ficus tree was overturned."

"What a mess," Aunt Tricia commented, eyeing the large dog. "And how long are you taking care of him?"

"Twelve more days," Hannah replied, pulling Sampson away from the marigolds he'd started to snack on. "But who's counting?" She looked worn out.

Turning to Lucy, she said, "Anyway, I was thinking I'd tire him out before tonight. Maybe with enough exercise he'll be too exhausted to chase Spooky, and I can get a good night's sleep. I remembered that park you have down the street, and I thought maybe you'd like to take a walk with us."

Her voice held a note of appeal, and Lucy tried to put her own weariness out of her mind. Hannah was a good friend, and she seemed to need cheering.

"Sure, I'm up for a short walk. But I'd like to be back within the hour."

Hannah grinned. "Great! We'll walk fast."

As they headed for the street, Aunt Tricia called after them. "Dinner in an hour! Hannah, you're welcome to stay."

47

Hannah turned around to reply. "Thanks, but we'll need to get home soon, anyway."

The pair walked down the sidewalk, their speed decided by the eighty-pound dog pulling them forward. Sampson seemed excited to be out and about, swiveling his head to take in all the sights and smells.

"Too bad I missed meeting Phoebe today," Hannah commented. "But I guess I'll meet her at the grand opening." She paused as Sampson was distracted by a patch of grass, snuffling enthusiastically.

"Yeah… she was really nice," Lucy glanced at Hannah. "But it was sort of odd. The minute I asked about her background, she seemed to shut down."

Hannah shrugged. "Not everyone has a past they want to remember."

She tightened her hold on Sampson's leash as they passed a woman walking a tiny poodle. The smaller dog growled, baring its teeth, while Sampson wagged his tail, looking confused. The woman didn't glance their way, moving on quickly.

"Sampson seemed friendly enough toward that dog," Lucy commented. "Are you sure he doesn't just want to get close to Spooky to scope her out? Maybe he really wants to be friends."

At that moment, a cat darted across an adjacent lawn, and Sampson exploded into a frenzy of barking, practically standing on his back legs as Hannah tried to keep him under control.

"No, Sampson!" she scolded him loudly, grabbing hold of his collar.

The cat disappeared from sight, and Sampson quieted, trotting down the street again.

"You see?" Hannah asked Lucy. "He's got a problem with cats."

"Hmm," Lucy eyed the shepherd thoughtfully. "I see what you mean."

As they passed a house with a teenage girl watering a flowerbed, Sampson's attention became riveted on the hose. He pulled sharply in that direction, and Hannah pulled him back to correct his course.

"Nope," she admonished in a strict voice. "Behave, Sampson!"

The warning did no good. When pulling forward didn't accomplish his goal, Sampson ducked his head, pulling backward. His collar slipped from his neck, and he was off at a gallop, heading right for the young lady.

"No! Come back!" Hannah cried out, running after him with the leash and collar in hand. "Sampson!"

The dog barreled right for the teenager, who shrieked and threw the hose aside.

A geyser of water shot up at the sky, cascading all over Lucy and Hannah as they neared the dog. Sampson took hold of the garden hose in his teeth, shaking it back and forth in a delighted frenzy, soaking everyone in its path.

Lucy managed to grab the hose as Hannah tackled Sampson, clutching him around the chest. "Drop it!"

Sampson complied, sitting down and grinning, eyes merry and coat saturated with water. Hannah slipped his collar back on, tightening it, and stepped back, apologizing to the girl, who had fled to the safety of her front porch.

"He's not my dog," she explained, as Sampson gave a violent shake, sending a fresh shower of droplets and dog hair in every direction. "I'm pet-sitting."

The girl nodded wordlessly, eyes wide.

Lucy and Hannah backtracked to the sidewalk, by unspoken agreement, heading back to Lucy's house.

Completely drenched and covered with wet dog hair, Hannah sighed, glancing over at Lucy, who was almost as disheveled. She offered Lucy a rueful grin.

"Well, that was enough excitement for one evening."

9

*L*ucy was rolling out Danish dough when Hannah arrived at the bakery the next morning.

"Did it work?" Lucy asked, smearing softened butter along the dough's surface before folding the dough over twice. "Did we wear out Sampson last night?"

Hannah shook her head, looking pained. "Only until about one in the morning. Then he crashed straight through the gate again and was after Spooky. I woke up to a horrendous screech coming from under the bed where she was hiding."

Lucy frowned, wishing she could help. "What did you do?"

Hannah tied on her apron and walked to the sink to wash her hands, answering over her shoulder. "I barricaded Sampson in the laundry room again and turned on my radio so I couldn't hear his barking."

"Wow." Lucy couldn't think of anything helpful to say. "Hmm."

Hannah shrugged, turning her attention to the daily list of products that needed baking posted on the kitchen's whiteboard.

"I'll start with the scones, unless you need something else first?"

Lucy shook her head, focused on rolling ropes of Danish dough into twisted figure-eights. "Sounds good to me."

The two worked in companionable silence for a time, and soon they heard Aunt Tricia coming through the front entrance. She peeked through the kitchen archway to say good morning.

"How did your soap sticks work out?" Hannah asked, dusting a tray of scones with coarse sugar before popping them into the oven.

Aunt Tricia looked triumphant. "Not a leaf disturbed," she boasted. "I think my garden's back on track."

Hearing this, Lucy knocked on a nearby wooden cutting board for luck. "Let's not jinx ourselves…"

Betsy arrived next and soon the bakery was bustling with regulars, stopping in on their way to work to grab a coffee and pastry. Lucy zipped back and forth between the back and front, replenishing trays, and enjoying seeing the familiar faces at the counter. A lot of the residents of Ivy Creek had been coming to Sweet Delights Bakery for years, even back to when it was run by Lucy's parents.

The bakery had all but cleared out of customers by eleven that morning, and Lucy was erasing the morning specials on the chalkboard when her eye was caught by an unfamiliar figure approaching.

The woman was tall and lean, dressed more fashionably than one normally saw in their little town, with gladiator style sandals showing off trim calves, and a white lace sleeveless dress with a high-low hem. Her hair was a dark auburn shade, with striking highlights accenting the trendy loose waves that fell just past her shoulders. She wore designer sunglasses, which she pushed up on her head upon entering the bakery.

She stood surveying the space, with her hands on her hips and her face absolutely devoid of expression.

Lucy greeted her with a smile, setting down the chalk. "Hello, there! Welcome to Sweet Delights Bakery."

The woman regarded her cooly, her green eyes framed by thick lashes and cat-eye kohl liner. "I assume you serve coffee?"

Lucy was a bit taken aback by the icy attitude, but managed to hang on to her smile.

"Of course. What can we get for you?" Lucy asked. Out of the corner of her eye, she saw Betsy step up to the counter, ready to serve.

The stranger approached the counter and spoke crisply to Betsy. "A Ristretto Doppio, please. To go."

Betsy gaped at her. "Um… I don't think we have that." She cast a panicked look at Lucy. "Do we?"

The customer let out a long-suffering sigh and rolled her eyes before Lucy had a chance to answer. "Of course, you don't. How about a double espresso with a dash of fat-free cream?"

Betsy nodded, her hands fumbling as she reached for a to go cup. "Is half and half OK?"

The woman looked bored, examining her fingernails, which were polished to perfection. "I suppose."

Betsy brewed her espresso, added a dash of half and half, and secured the lid, passing the cup across the counter. "Would you like to add a pastry to that?"

The woman raised a finger for silence, sipping her coffee experimentally. She frowned, obviously displeased. "Truly disappointing. What kind of coffee beans are you using?"

Betsy's mouth opened and closed, resembling a fish on a hook, and Lucy decided enough was enough. She stepped over to join her young employee, who had turned red with embarrassment.

"We use a blend of arabica and robusta." Lucy held out a hand, introducing herself.

"I'm Lucy Hale, the owner."

The woman looked amused by the gesture. She ignored Lucy's hand but inclined her head, introducing herself.

"Camille Ashton. I've recently relocated here to work for Phoebe's Bridal Shop as a runway and catalogue model. Since I'll be living in Ivy Creek now, it would be helpful if you could begin carrying my preferred coffee."

Lucy was a bit taken aback by the request, which had been stated more like a demand. "And what coffee would that be?" she inquired.

Camille offered a thin smile. "Wollenford Jamaican Blue Mountain."

Lucy shook her head, familiar with the variety, which sold for well over a hundred dollars a pound. "I'm afraid, here in Ivy Creek, we don't have enough interest in high-end coffee to warrant carrying that brand."

Camille compressed her lips, abandoning her cup on the counter. "That's a shame," she said. Without another word, she turned and headed for the door.

As she approached the exit, a man was walking up the sidewalk, preparing to enter the bakery. Lucy watched as his eyes widened, getting a look at Camille. He nearly walked into the glass as he rushed to open the door for her, admiring her openly as she strutted through with barely a glance in his direction. Turning his head, he followed her with his eyes as she folded her long, elegant form into a sleek sports car.

She zoomed out of the parking lot, and the man turned back around. His eyes were still dazed as he walked forward, straight up to the counter where Lucy stood with Betsy.

"If either of you know that woman's name, I'd be grateful if you shared it. I've never believed in love at first sight until now..."

He paused. Betsy stared at him, wide eyed, as he made the following pronouncement, with utmost sincerity. "I believe I've just met my future wife."

Lucy couldn't help but smile at the romantic statement. "That would be Camille Ashton, a model for Phoebe's Bridal Shop, opening soon."

The man lowered his eyelids, reverently repeating, "Camille... Camille..." Opening his eyes again, he looked at the ladies with a sheepish grin. "I'm sorry. What a thing to say to total strangers. You both must think I'm a lunatic."

"Not at all," Betsy assured him, a smile curving her lips. "I think that's the most romantic thing I've ever heard."

He offered her a grateful smile, then looked from one to the other. "I'm here on behalf of Classic Fare. My boss said you guys were lending us some almond flour. By the way, my name's Dale Crane."

"Hi, Dale. Nice to meet you," replied Lucy. "Give me just a second. I have five pounds bagged up for you."

She zipped into the back, where Aunt Tricia was assisting Hannah with the bagging of apple-cinnamon bread. "Need any help out front?" her aunt inquired.

"Nope, we're good," Lucy assured her, grabbing the bag of flour she'd set aside.

When she returned to the counter, Dale and Betsy were chatting about the upcoming bridal show.

"Well, good luck," Dale said to Betsy, accepting the package from Lucy with a thank you. "I hope you find a great wedding dress! Maybe I'll see you there."

"Thanks, see you around!" Betsy called out as he walked toward the door.

She waited until the door had closed behind him before turning to Lucy with eyebrows raised. "Can you believe that Camille person's attitude? I swear, icicles formed on the ceiling while she was standing here."

Lucy chuckled. "She seemed rather full of herself," she agreed. Her eyes followed Dale as he walked to Classic Fare's delivery van.

"I hope Dale Crane knows what he's getting into."

10

Several days later, Lucy and Hannah were hard at work on Melanie Cameron's wedding cake. Hannah expertly piped scrollwork around the sides of the iced layers while Lucy carefully stacked the tiers on top of each other, securing them in place with a sharpened wooden dowel rod that ran through all the layers.

"So, Lucy…" Hannah ventured, looking up from her work. "I think I'm ready to admit defeat."

Lucy stepped back to eye the stacked tiers, ensuring that everything was level.

"How's that?" she asked distractedly, making a small adjustment.

Hannah switched pastry tips on her icing bag, moving on to pipe a pearl-like border along the top and bottom edges.

"With Spooky and Sampson," she clarified. She glanced at Lucy, catching her eye. "I need your help."

"Sure," Lucy answered. "What do you need?" She felt sorry for her friend. With her sweet nature, Hannah had gotten in over her head, offering to take care of Joseph's dog.

Hannah paused, folding her pastry bag down to refill it with vanilla buttercream icing.

"Could you possibly let Spooky stay at your house until Joseph comes back? You know I wouldn't ask if I wasn't desperate."

Lucy's heart went out to her. She knew how much it cost her friend to ask. Hannah would be making a sacrifice, too, being separated from Spooky for days on end.

"Of course," she agreed. "I'm sure Gigi and Spooky will be fine together."

The two felines had met previously, when Hannah had first adopted Spooky last Halloween. She'd brought her to Lucy's house so the cats could meet. Gigi had been a little aloof but curious. The cats seemed wary of each other, but neither had displayed hostility.

"Oh, thank you," Hannah said with relief. "I could really use some peace at my house."

The ladies finished their task and Lucy prepared a kit with spatulas, scissors, and icing bags to bring on their delivery. The cake needed a fresh flower topper, which they would create on site.

A few minutes later, the pair loaded the three-tier wedding cake into a foam core box, carefully carrying it out to the delivery van.

"Ready?" Lucy asked, and Hannah nodded, hopping into the passenger seat. The cake was going to The Highlands

Country Club, a ritzy venue about ten minutes away. Lucy drove slowly, watching out for any bumps in the road. Transporting tiered cakes was a stressful, but necessary, part of the job.

A short while later, they were passing through the stone walls and wrought-iron gates of the exclusive club. Lucy drove around the building to the back parking lot. They propped open the doors of the banquet room's service entrance and returned to the van, carefully carrying the boxed cake together, walking sideways. The pair had delivered many wedding cakes as a team, and by now had their routine down pat.

Once inside the venue, Lucy looked around, locating the cake table. They gently set the box down. Hannah returned to the van for their bag of tools while Lucy eased the cake out from the box.

Once she'd centered the wedding cake in place on the table, she relaxed. The hard part was done, and she felt the tension leave her shoulders.

Glancing around the immense room, Lucy saw many familiar faces - the industry professionals hard at work. She waved a greeting at the sound technician as he tapped the mic, and then exchanged smiles with the venue's coordinator, who stood on the sidelines, ready to help. The catering staff was busy setting up tables, with servers crisscrossing paths while carrying covered silver trays.

Hannah came back with their tools just as Lucy spotted her friend Deanna, who ran Bountiful Blooms florist shop. Deanna turned around in response to Lucy's greeting and hurried over to them.

"Hello, ladies!" Deanna said with a warm smile, then turned to admire the cake. "Another stunning design, I see. You two are the best."

She located a cardboard box that had been set underneath the cake table's flowing satin skirts, and straightened up, handing it to Lucy. "Here are your flowers for the topper. Will you need some additional greenery?"

Lucy pawed through the pink roses, baby's breath, and ferns nestled in the box and shook her head. "I think this will cover it. Thanks, Deanna." She set the box down and began to clip stems, chatting with the florist as she worked.

"How's business?"

Deanna watched as Lucy arranged flowers into two piles on the table, according to size. "Booming! All the buzz about that new bridal shop opening up seems to have lit a fire under this year's brides-to-be! I've had back-to-back appointments all week. How about you guys?"

"We're slammed, too," Hannah confirmed. "I think Phoebe's shop is going to be good for us all. Are you attending the grand opening?"

Deanna nodded cheerfully. "I wouldn't miss it for the world! Although, I have to say, I was disappointed to learn Sweet Delights won't be catering it. Did you guys bid on it?"

Lucy shook her head, piping a mound of buttercream on the top tier. She began to choose flowers, inserting them at angles into the icing. "I think Classic Fare was locked in ahead of time. I never heard a word about any bidding. It's probably for the best, though. We're super busy right now."

Deanna leaned forward, lowering her voice conspiratorially. "I've a bit of juicy gossip…"

Hannah grinned. "Do tell." She began arranging rose petals in a circle around the cake platter.

Deanna glanced around to make sure she wasn't being overheard. "Well… I'm not sure if you're aware, but Phoebe's Bridal Shop has employed several fashion models. Not only for the grand opening show, but for other showcase events and catalog work."

Lucy tucked a few sprigs of baby's breath in between flowers, remarking dryly, "Yes, I've recently made the acquaintance of one of the models. She was rather rude, expecting me to stock Jamaican Blue Mountain coffee beans from Wollenford now that she's in town."

Hannah shook her head, having already heard the story. "I still can't believe that. I don't see how anyone could afford that stuff, even a model."

Deanna speculated. "That wouldn't have been Camille Ashton, would it?"

Lucy glanced at her, surprised. "Yes, it was. How did you guess?"

Deanna chuckled. "That's who my little tidbit is about. I haven't met her myself, but she certainly made an impression on Dale Crane. You may not know him, but he's a chef—"

Lucy finished the sentence for her. "Employed by Jackson Louis at Classic Fare. Yes, Dale and Camille met at my bakery. Well… not so much met, as Dale nearly fell at her feet, love-struck, while Camille declined to even notice him."

Deanna's eyes sparkled merrily. "I bet she's noticing him now. For the past three days he's had a standing order of a dozen long-stemmed roses delivered to her apartment each day."

Hannah's eyes widened. "Wow, that's got to add up to some major bucks!"

Deanna nodded. "Apparently, he's determined to win her over. Each delivery has a romantic line of poetry included on a notecard. She certainly made an impression on him."

Lucy shook her head, mystified. *All that from just one look, not even a conversation between the two.*

"How long is he planning to keep that up?" Hannah wondered out loud.

Deanna's answer was exactly what Lucy would have guessed, given Dale's declaration at the bakery.

"He says as long as it takes. Until Camille agrees to go out with him."

---

11

*L*ucy rubbed her eyes and yawned, shuffling into the kitchen. It was rare that she rose earlier than Aunt Tricia, but, given that her aunt's book club meeting last night had run until nine o'clock, it was no wonder she was catching a few more winks.

On autopilot, Lucy retrieved a cat treat for Gigi, then moved to the counter to brew a pot of coffee. After standing for five minutes in a sleepy daze, watching the magical elixir drip into the pot, she was rewarded with her first sip of the steaming beverage while standing at the kitchen window.

The sun had just begun to light the day. Lucy's eyes roamed over the soft summer colors slowly being illuminated, contentedly watching the birds flit from tree to tree.

Her gaze came to rest on the vegetable garden, and suddenly widened.

"Oh, no!"

Her mouth dropped open in shock, and she set her cup down, rushing to yank open the back door.

Barefoot, she stood on the brick patio, dismayed by the scene before her. The vegetable garden once again lay in ruin, stalks bent and missing leaves, forlorn and twisting at odd angles. The ground was dug up, with furrows running haphazardly this way and that, as though an army of insane groundhogs had been let loose.

"So much for Chloe Barnes's advice..." Lucy mumbled, noting the soap skewers had been knocked from their stakes. Bits of soap littered the area, some laying in place beneath the sharpened sticks, while others were several feet away. One soap cube even lay at the edge of the brick.

Lucy bent to pick it up and let it go immediately, grimacing in disgust. It was slimy.

Good grief! Had something tried to eat it?

With a sigh, she straightened, not relishing the idea of informing Aunt Tricia that their diligent efforts had all been for naught.

Suddenly, Lucy heard a shriek of dismay coming from the kitchen.

"No! Not again!"

Apparently, as the bearer of bad news, she was off the hook.

Aunt Tricia was up.

————

"Now, this is supposed to be foolproof," Aunt Tricia informed Lucy, as they stood in the garden, threading string through holes punched in aluminum pie tins. "I found it online in a gardening article. Both the reflective surface and the sound the pans make rattling will scare off all wildlife."

Lucy tied a loop of string around a bamboo post and attached a pie pan. "If you say so. Me, I'm thinking maybe we should just focus on growing summer squash. For whatever reason, the animals aren't bothering the squash plants."

Aunt Tricia ignored her suggestion, continuing to relay her findings. "I also read this morning that raccoons are attracted to soap. I bet it was raccoons that knocked down the stakes and tried to steal the soap."

"By carrying it in their mouths?" Lucy wondered out loud, still disgusted by the slimy soap shard she'd tried to pick up.

Aunt Tricia gave her an odd look. "Of course, in their mouths! They use their little hands and feet to walk, don't they?"

Lucy mumbled, "I guess so." She frowned. "Why do they like soap?"

"They like anything unusual. Raccoons hoard whatever they consider being a treasure."

The ladies finished tying the pie pans, and next set about driving the bamboo poles into the soft ground around the garden. The breeze immediately sent the pie tins flying about, clattering noisily as they crashed into one another.

"That should do it," Aunt Tricia announced with satisfaction.

"I sure hope so," Lucy answered. *This year's garden was sure requiring a lot of time and effort.*

"I'm going to run by Zander's and pick up more vegetable flats. Do you want to join me?" Aunt Tricia asked.

Lucy consulted her watch. "I'll stay here. Hannah said she'll be bringing Spooky over by late morning." Sweet Delights was closed today, and it was just as well. Lucy was feeling tired, dirty, and out of sorts. She decided a quick shower was in order.

Just after eleven o'clock, Lucy heard a knock on the door. She peeked through the living room window, seeing Hannah's car in the drive.

Opening the door, she welcomed her friend inside, noting the large cat carrier which held a softly complaining Spooky.

"Poor girl is terrified," Hannah said, setting the carrier down. "Her whole world has been turned upside-down." She unlatched the carrier's gate, and Spooky cautiously poked her head out.

"Hi there, baby," Lucy crooned, bending down. "It's your Aunt Lucy. You remember me, don't you?" She held out her hand.

Spooky sniffed it and rubbed the side of her face against Lucy's knuckles, purring.

Hannah looked relieved. "Thanks so much for agreeing to help, Lucy. I don't think I could stand another night of playing referee."

Lucy straightened up with a smile. "It's no trouble at all, Hannah. What are your plans for the day?"

Hannah glanced out the window at her car, where Sampson peered hopefully through the windshield. "I'm taking Sampson to run in the park, and then I need to straighten up at home. My apartment looks like a disaster zone."

A bark followed her comment, and Hannah winced. "Someone's getting impatient."

She crouched down, speaking to Spooky, who was exploring the living room. "It's going to be OK, little one. Lucy is going to take good care of you, and Mama will be back to get you when the big, bad doggy is gone."

Another bark sounded, and Hannah straightened. "I should go before your neighbors get annoyed. Thanks a million, Lucy! I owe you one."

Lucy shut the door behind her friend and sat down, cross-legged on the carpet, watching Spooky roam around the room.

"Gigi," she called softly. "Come greet your visitor."

A few minutes later, Gigi trotted into the room, sniffing the air. Tail swishing with interest, Spooky approached the Persian, crouching nearby and lowering her head.

A submissive posture, Lucy noted. *That was good.* It was important for Gigi to know that Spooky was not challenging her.

Gigi's ears flattened as she regarded her visitor distrustfully. Sidestepping, she backed from the room, heading toward the kitchen. Spooky watched her leave, then scurried after her, keeping low to the ground.

Lucy followed them into the kitchen, quickly filling a bowl of dry food for Spooky. She set it down on the far side of the room, calling Spooky to her. She didn't want Gigi to feel her food supply was being threatened.

Spooky trotted over, sniffing the bowl and finding it acceptable. She began to delicately nibble, keeping a close watch on Gigi.

"There you go, girl," Lucy said softly.

Seeing her favorite human paying too much attention to the interloper did not sit well with Gigi. She abandoned her bowl, stalking over to Spooky, her hackles raised. Pushing her face into Spooky's bowl, the feline gave a low growl of warning, shocking Lucy.

"Gigi, stop that immediately!" she scolded. "You have your own food." She picked up Gigi, crossing the room and setting her down in front of her food bowl.

"This one's yours."

With a withering look, Gigi stalked out of the kitchen, turning back at the threshold to hiss at Spooky.

Lucy sighed, exasperated. The two had met previously and gotten along fine.

Why did Gigi have to act up now?

12

*L*ucy was exhausted the next morning, having had her own taste of what Hannah had been going through. All night long, she'd been intermittently woken by Gigi's hisses and growls as the Persian warned Spooky away from Lucy's bedroom. The pair hadn't actually been involved in a skirmish yet, but she had to feel bad for poor Spooky.

She gave Gigi a good talking to, sitting cross-legged on the living room floor, after watching her normally sweet-tempered kitty once again terrorize their visitor when she came out of hiding. Spooky had fled down the hallway, taking cover under the bed in the guest room.

"Listen, now," Lucy commanded, looking into Gigi's yellow eyes. "You're going to have to put up with having Spooky here, just for a week or so. It would go easier on all of us if you weren't so territorial."

Gigi regarded her owner with a dubious gaze before turning her back and swishing her tail.

Lucy sighed and stood up, her body weary from lack of sleep. She tightened her bathrobe and put on her slippers, stepping out to the front walkway to retrieve the newspaper.

As she carried it back inside, she noticed the bold print of the headline.

Ivy Creek's Hometown Girl Returns – Vanna Verity Attending Grand Opening Event

Lucy scanned the article as she sipped her coffee. Apparently, Vanna had arrived the day before, along with her entourage, including a Mr. Tate McQueen–her much younger fiancé who was currently starring in a popular soap opera on TV.

Aunt Tricia walked into the kitchen, immediately going to the window to look outside at her garden.

"The pie pans seem to be working," she commented. "Everything is still standing."

"Mm-hmm…" Lucy's nose was still buried in the newspaper.

"What are you reading?" Her aunt put the kettle on for her morning tea, sitting down across from Lucy.

"Vanna Verity has arrived, as of yesterday," Lucy murmured. "They're sure making a big deal out of it. She has appearances scheduled at the library, the high school, and even at the town hall for a photo op with the mayor. All that before Phoebe's Grand Opening on Saturday."

Aunt Tricia mused, "I wonder if she'll stop by the bakery."

Lucy looked up, curious. "Are you a fan, Auntie?"

The kettle whistled, and Aunt Tricia rose, filling her mug and plopping in a tea bag before rejoining Lucy at the table.

She shrugged. "It would be interesting to see her. She hasn't been on the air for quite a while now."

Lucy lay down the newspaper, looking at the clock. "Either way, you'll see her soon enough at the bridal show. I know Betsy's really looking forward to it. Hannah, too."

Her aunt snorted. "Hannah said she's only going to get a glimpse of that McQueen fellow Vanna's engaged to."

Lucy chuckled. "I wouldn't be surprised if that was the motivation for a lot of the ladies planning to attend."

———

THE TOWN certainly was ramped up about Vanna's visit, Lucy thought, driving into work. There were homemade banners hung on several storefronts, proclaiming, "Welcome Back, Vanna!", and she even spotted a sign in front of the sub shop advertising the "Vanna Verity Special".

Amused, Lucy wondered what had prompted the celebrity to visit her hometown again. Was it really just to support the opening of Phoebe's Bridal Shop? Or were the cynical comments she'd overheard at Bing's Grocery closer to the mark—that this was all staged to breathe life into Vanna's dying career?

As she opened the door to the bakery, she saw Hannah and Betsy engaged in conversation.

"Good morning," Betsy greeted her. "I was just saying to Hannah that maybe we should create a new dessert in Vanna Verity's honor. The regulars would probably go for it—everyone seems super excited she's here."

Hannah interjected, "But what dessert starts with V? That's a tough one."

Lucy thought for a moment. "Vanilla cupcakes?"

Hannah made a face. "Vanilla is boring."

Betsy's brow wrinkled. "There's got to be something."

Lucy opened the register to stock the till. "Let it marinate for a bit. We'll think of something."

The ladies went about the business of opening up the shop, and Aunt Tricia arrived just a few minutes later, reporting that her garden was still unmolested.

"Victory!" Betsy cheered, then her eyes opened wide. "Vanna's Victory Cheesecake?" She looked at Lucy, eyebrows raised.

Aunt Tricia looked confused. "What did I miss?'

Lucy chuckled. "We're trying to come up with a dessert in Vanna's honor."

"Ah," the older woman commented, furrowing her brows. "Vanna's vanilla cream puffs?"

Hannah loudly booed her. "No more vanilla names, please," she requested.

The bell jangled, letting in a customer, and the ladies slipped quickly into professional mode.

"Welcome to Sweet Delights Bakery," Betsy greeted the patron. "How are you this morning?"

The woman hesitated before venturing timidly, "Um... thank you. I'm good, I guess."

She was short in stature, dressed in a businesslike, but comfortable-looking, skirt and suit jacket with flat heels. She appeared to be in her twenties, with medium brown hair cut into a bob just below her ears. She nervously fiddled with the buttons on her blazer as she surveyed the pastry case, chewing at her bottom lip.

"Are you new in town?" Lucy asked curiously, not recognizing her. "I'm the owner, Lucy Hale."

The woman gave a quick nod, offering a tight, cheerless smile. "I'm Debbie Ritner," she said. "Pleased to meet you. I'm Vanna Verity's personal assistant."

Betsy's eyes widened. "Is she here?" She stood on tiptoe, peering out at the parking lot.

Ms. Ritner shook her head. "She's at the hotel, having a massage. I've been instructed to pick up some snacks to keep on hand… but… I don't know what to get."

She looked despairingly at the pastry case, stocked with a variety of muffins, turnovers, brownies, cookies, and cupcakes.

"Do you have any vegan desserts?" she asked timidly. "Vanna's a strict vegan."

Aunt Tricia pointed to the turnovers at the end of the case. "These are vegan. We use vegetable shortening in the dough instead of butter," she explained.

"And the no-bake chocolate oatmeal cookies, too," Hannah chimed in. "No egg or butter."

Ms. Ritner tapped her lip anxiously. "She is also allergic to gluten…"

73

Before more suggestions were made, Lucy interceded, familiar with Ms. Verity's dietary preferences. "And also, no refined sugar, is that correct?" She remembered Jackson Louis telling her that.

Ms. Ritner nodded, reluctantly dragging her eyes from the decadent chocolate cheesecake bars. She sighed, looking hungry. "Yes. Vegan, gluten-free, and no refined sugar. I don't suppose you have anything like that?"

Lucy shook her head, regretting she hadn't seen this situation coming. She simply hadn't expected Vanna to send her assistant into a bakery for snacks, given the star's restricted diet.

"I'm afraid not," she said apologetically. "At least, not dessert items. The only thing we have that fits those parameters is fruit salad–"

Ms. Ritner shook her head, looking worried. "No, no, that won't do. She specifically wanted dessert-type items." She drummed her fingertips on the counter, fretting.

"Oh, my. I'm not sure what to do. I hate to go back empty-handed. Would there happen to be another bakery in this town?"

Lucy bit her lip, feeling sorry for the woman. She had a sudden thought.

"Not another bakery, but Rick's Café might have something. Betsy, didn't we see a sugar-free vegan dessert on the menu when we had lunch there?"

Betsy brightened, nodding her head. "I think so… something to do with bananas?"

Lucy snapped her fingers. "That's it." She turned to Ms. Ritner. "It was banana pudding. A sugar-free, vegan variety, and banana pudding wouldn't have gluten, either."

Ms. Ritner looked hopeful. "Oh, that would be great! Can you give me directions, please?"

"Sure," Lucy said, flipping over an order sheet to scribble a map. She looked up. "If you leave me your business card, Ms. Ritner, we can whip up something later and give you a call. It's always good to have options."

Ms. Ritner offered a small smile, her anxious expression finally relaxing. "Thank you so much." She fished in her purse, laying her card on the counter.

A few minutes later, Vanna's assistant was on her way, the doorbell jangling behind her.

Lucy turned to her crew.

"Ladies, besides a catchy name starting with V, we really need to come up with a special that Vanna, herself, can actually eat! Let's put our thinking caps on."

13

"So, what did you guys come up with?" Taylor asked, as he and Lucy walked hand-in-hand, on their way to dinner. He'd been highly entertained by her story of meeting Vanna's assistant.

Lucy grinned at him as they approached the restaurant.

"Vanna's Vegan Carrot Cake Squares," she announced. "Using almond flour and agave syrup."

Taylor opened the heavy double doors of McIntyre's Steakhouse, allowing her to pass through first. "No cream cheese icing, I suppose?"

Lucy giggled. "Nope. Iced with coconut sugar glaze." She peered into the dining room, seeing it was only half full, while Taylor gave their name to the hostess.

"Right this way, please," the pleasant young woman instructed, leading them into the far end of the grand room.

Lucy took in the burgundy leather booths, recessed lighting, and old-fashioned, thick, bubble-glass windows. A rush of satisfaction enveloped her. She loved McIntyre's. She and Taylor tried to make a point of coming here once per season.

Taylor held her chair for her and requested a bottle of red wine. They perused the menus in comfortable silence, the faint strains of classical music adding to the ambience.

Lucy decided on Fettuccini Alfredo, and Taylor, the rib-eye and a baked potato. The server took their order and poured their wine, promising to return shortly with their food.

Taylor reached across the table, taking Lucy's hand. "Did I tell you how lovely you look tonight?" His blue eyes were intense, and Lucy shivered pleasantly, basking in his attention.

"You're not so bad yourself," she teased softly, squeezing his hand.

She'd been prone to fits of nostalgia ever since Georgio's Pizza had closed, and now she could almost see Taylor as he was back then, as a boy of sixteen. *How far we've come*, she thought. *And yet here we are, in the same place.*

They sipped their wine, and Lucy glanced around the room at the other patrons. A familiar head of glossy auburn caught her attention and she squinted at the table in a far corner, recognizing the couple.

"That's Camille Ashton and Dale Crane," she whispered excitedly. "I guess Dale's efforts finally won her over." *Wait until I tell Hannah*, she thought.

Taylor cocked his head, puzzled. "Who?"

Lucy leaned forward, speaking in a low tone. "That model I told you about, who wanted the expensive coffee. Dale was the guy who came in right when she was leaving, claiming it was love at first sight, remember?"

"Ah, yes," Taylor said, glancing at the couple, who looked to be involved in a deep conversation, heads bent close. "Well, good for him. I hope it works out."

He looked back at Lucy with a grin.

"We men sometimes have to be patient to get what we want."

Lucy chuckled. *Patient was not the first word that came to mind when she thought of Taylor. Tenacious, yes, but patient, not so much.*

———

THE ALARM CLOCK went off far too early for Lucy's liking, and she rolled over, hiding her head under the covers, trying to muffle the sound. When that failed, she bopped it with a pillow, one eye open, feeling cranky. It continued to ring, and she was forced to fully awaken, leaning over to slam her hand down on the button.

Blessed silence reigned for less than a minute before a loud feline screech was heard coming from the hallway. *Spooky*, she realized, frowning when Gigi's answering growl sounded immediately after. *Darn it!*

Hopping out of bed, she slipped into her robe and scurried to the hallway, hoping the feuding felines hadn't woken her aunt.

Spooky had fled the hallway, and Gigi sat complacently at the entrance to the kitchen, fluffy white tail curled neatly around her feet. She blinked innocently at Lucy.

"You're not fooling anyone," Lucy informed her. "I heard your tone. That is no way to treat our visitor."

"Oh, good, you're awake," she heard her aunt call from the kitchen. "The pair of them have been going at it for an hour."

Lucy entered the kitchen, apologizing. "I'm so sorry, Auntie. Did they wake you up?"

Aunt Tricia was sitting at the table with a cup of tea and a half-finished bagel in front of her. "No, I actually woke up with the clanging of those darn pie pans–which, I might add, did not keep the deer from feasting on my sprouts, no matter what the internet article said. Hogwash!"

"Oh, no!" Lucy rushed to the window. The garden had been desecrated again, but she didn't think it looked completely demolished this time. "I think it can be salvaged," she said, hoping to soothe her aunt. "And look at the summer squash. It's already flowering!"

Aunt Tricia harrumphed. "That's a good thing, I guess, seeing as the rest of the plants don't stand a chance. When did our neighborhood deer and rabbits become such voracious feeders?"

The phone rang, and Lucy quickly turned to answer it, grateful for the distraction. *Between the cats fighting and the deer chomping, Aunt Tricia appeared to be out of sorts this morning.*

"Hello?"

Hannah's voice greeted her, sounding out of breath. "Lucy? It's me, Hannah. I'm afraid I'm going to be late. Probably by an hour or so." She half-covered the phone, and Lucy heard her sternly admonishing, "No, you stay! Right there. I mean it! Stay."

"What's up?" Lucy asked, concerned. She hoped Hannah wasn't having more behavioral problems with Sampson–she'd thought taking Spooky off her friend's hands would have solved the problem.

"It's Sampson," Hannah moaned. "I let him out for a romp in the yard, and you wouldn't guess what he did!"

"Did he, ah… bother a neighbor's cat?" Lucy guessed.

"Worse," Hannah replied. "Much worse. He tangled with a skunk. Now he stinks to high heaven. I didn't even want to let him back in the apartment, but I don't have an outdoor water source here. I really, really, need to bathe him. I'm sorry. I'll be there as soon as I can."

"OK," Lucy assured her, wincing at the mental image. "No worries, I'll start the baking."

She hung up the phone, just as Spooky raced past her like the devil was after her, fluffed out to twice her normal size.

Gigi strolled into the kitchen seconds later, serenely sitting in front of her treat cabinet, innocent by all appearances.

"You don't know how good you've got it," Lucy told her, fetching the Persian her morning treat, before sitting down to relay Hannah's situation to Aunt Tricia.

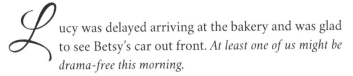ucy was delayed arriving at the bakery and was glad to see Betsy's car out front. *At least one of us might be drama-free this morning.*

Before she'd left home, she'd been forced to separate Spooky and Gigi, after their constant racing about had knocked over a lamp in the guest room. She'd closeted Gigi in her own bedroom, with food and water and a makeshift litter box, reasoning the Persian would be enraged if Spooky spent the day in her owner's inner sanctum.

"Where's Hannah?" Betsy asked, as Lucy walked through the door.

Lucy filled her in on Sampson's escapade, and Betsy shook her head, trying not to laugh.

"Oh, poor Hannah. I hope she leaves her windows open."

Lucy poured herself a coffee and tied her apron around her waist. "And Aunt Tricia hasn't had the greatest morning, either. The deer and rabbits have been in the garden again, despite the pie pans."

Betsy looked thoughtful. "I can't remember exactly what it is, but there's an old country trick to keep the wildlife away." She scrunched her face up, thinking, but then shook her head. "Maybe it will come to me later."

Lucy wrote the morning specials on the chalkboard. "I hope it works better than red pepper, soap shards, or pie pans. We're running out of options."

She looked over her shoulder at Betsy, who was cleaning the front window.

"How are the wedding plans going? Have things calmed down a bit with your mom?"

Betsy shook her head, her face looking glum. "I never would have thought planning a happy event would have the potential to make so many people mad. Now my aunt and uncle want to invite another ten people–friends of theirs that I don't even know! I hate to sound penny-pinching, but we have to keep our guest list to a reasonable amount. I don't think my aunt is aware that the caterer charges by the head."

"Perhaps you should explain that to her," Lucy advised.

Betsy finished cleaning the windows and returned to the counter, stowing the supplies underneath. "I don't dare. If she knew what the caterer was charging for the food, she'd start telling my mother they should do all the cooking themselves."

They heard Hannah arrive through the back entrance, and a moment later, she rounded the corner, coming through the archway. She looked exhausted.

"I don't think the stink is ever going to come off Sampson," she announced glumly. "I scrubbed him three times, and he still smells skunky. And now my apartment does, too."

"Maybe you should douse him with perfume," Betsy suggested.

Hannah stared at her. "Perfume? Have you met me? I don't own any perfume."

Lucy smirked, turning as the bell jangled. It was Aunt Tricia.

The older woman took in Hannah's appearance. "You look like you lost a fight," she observed.

Hannah replied crossly, pouring an extra-large coffee for herself. "I did. The skunk won. Sampson reeks, even after multiple shampooing."

"Tomato juice," Aunt Tricia said, earning puzzled looks all around.

"Pardon?" Hannah looked confused.

"Have none of you heard of that before?" Aunt Tricia looked over the top of her spectacles. "Buy a big jug of tomato juice on the way home. Give Sampson a bath with it. Scrub it into his fur just like shampoo, then rinse it off. It really works. I remember growing up, my uncle had a couple of hunting dogs who used to tangle with skunks. Tomato juice is the only thing that gets the stink out."

Hannah looked hopeful. "Thanks, Tricia. It sounds weird, but hey, what have I got to lose?"

The crew got to work, each concentrating on their own individual tasks. Between customers, Betsy worked on a colorful banner advertising their new product, "Vanna's Vegan Carrot Cake Squares", generating a lot of interest.

Before long, Hannah was forced to reorder her baking list for the day, baking a second round of the new dessert, as they were perilously close to selling out.

Just after midday, Lucy received a phone call from Phoebe Pierce.

"Hi, Lucy, could I ask you a favor?"

"Of course," Lucy replied, holding the phone between her ear and shoulder as she switched the mixer to second speed. She was making a double batch of glaze for the carrot cake squares, guessing that their popularity would continue.

"Do you have any folding tables? I'm looking for something around six feet long to set my brochures and catalogs on for the show."

Lucy was happy to help. The buzz Phoebe's Bridal Shop was creating around town had certainly pushed their bakery revenue up for this month.

"I sure do," she replied. "And I'll be downtown tomorrow. I can drop it off if you like."

Phoebe sounded pleased. "That would be great, if you don't mind. Thanks, Lucy. See you tomorrow."

They both hung up, and Lucy replaced the phone on the charger.

She'd been dying for a peek inside the old Georgio's Pizza to see what Phoebe had done with the space.

———

THE DAY FLEW BY, and before too long, Lucy was pulling back into her own driveway. They'd been so busy all day, she'd barely had time to think about the situation with Spooky and Gigi. Now that she was home, she wondered what she could do to help the pair get along.

Aunt Tricia was already home, having left the bakery an hour before closing. Lucy had seen her in a close conference with Betsy just before she'd left and had assumed Betsy was sharing her wedding planning woes.

She pushed open the front door, calling out, "I'm home!"

Immediately, there was a loud, pitiful howl coming from the direction of her bedroom. Lucy recognized Gigi's unhappy voice and hurried over to release the Persian from her prison.

"I'm sorry, baby-" she apologized as she opened the door. Gigi streaked past her, having had enough of being locked away.

Lucy started to follow her, hoping to get back in her kitty's good graces by means of a cat treat, when her eyes took in the state of her bedroom.

She stood, horrified, in the doorway, mouth half open in shock.

Gigi had been busy. The room looked like a tornado had hit. One curtain hung haphazardly from its rod as though it had been climbed. The bookshelf was half-empty, with paperbacks and knick-knacks scattered all over the carpet. The worst destruction was focused on the bed.

Lucy's favorite down-filled pillow had been shredded to bits, and small white feathers littered the coverlet and nightstand.

Lucy closed her eyes briefly before decisively shutting the door. She needed to unwind before she could even begin to deal with this.

She turned on her heel and walked toward the kitchen, in search of a glass of wine. *Spooky must be in hiding*, she thought, seeing Gigi lounging insolently across the kitchen threshold.

Stepping over her, Lucy narrowed her eyes. "Don't even think about asking for a you-know-what. I saw what you did to my bedroom."

Gigi yawned, swishing her tail, apparently unconcerned.

Lucy suddenly spotted Aunt Tricia through the kitchen window, walking slowly around the perimeter of the garden, holding a paper shopping bag. She poured herself a glass of wine and let herself out through the back door.

"Hi, Auntie. What are you doing?" Puzzled, she watched as Aunt Tricia reached into the bag and came up with a handful of… something. She distributed it over the ground, moving a few feet and repeating the procedure. "What is that?"

Aunt Tricia looked up. "Human hair."

Lucy was flabbergasted. "What? Why? And where did you get it?"

Aunt Tricia scattered another handful over the earth. "Betsy told me about it. I guess it's an old gardener's trick. Human hair around the perimeter of a garden will deter wildlife. I stopped at the barbershop on the way home."

Lucy shook her head, marveling at how many gardening *tricks* were in existence, and none of them seemed to work.

She was doubtful that this newest one would prove any different.

She sipped her wine, determined to relax, her eye caught by the single healthy plant flourishing in the corner of the garden.

Maybe they'd be better served planting only summer squash next year.

15

*L*ucy drove through Ivy Creek's downtown area the next afternoon, on her way to Phoebe's shop. She had to smile at the number of banners she spotted along her route, welcoming Vanna–apparently, not everyone in Ivory Creek shared the cynical attitude of the women she'd encountered at Bing's Grocery. It really seemed that the majority of the town's residents were excited that their *Hometown Queen* was gracing them with a visit.

She pulled into a parking spot in front of the shop, noticing immediately how Phoebe had transformed the space. The front window was now dressed with gauzy white curtains, opened to reveal a mannequin wearing a stunning, beaded, ivory wedding gown. White silk flowers were scattered across a sky-blue satin cloth that served as a floor dressing, and script lettering in the same sky-blue was stenciled on the glass proclaiming: **Phoebe's Bridal Shop.**

Lucy smiled. Seeing the old commercial space refreshed went a long way in soothing her melancholy over Georgio's Pizza's demise.

She got out of her SUV, opening the back to retrieve the folding table she'd promised Phoebe. It wasn't heavy so much as awkward, and Lucy lugged it over to the entrance, propping it against the wall as she opened the glass door, holding it in place with her hip.

The shop's main room was deserted, but Lucy could hear voices coming from the back. Assuming Phoebe was busy assisting a customer, she left the table leaning against the front wall and wandered about, marveling at the variety of gowns that were already displayed on elegantly posed mannequins.

Some of the dresses were quite fancy, but when Lucy peeked, searching for a price tag, she was unable to locate one. Hopefully, Betsy would be able to find a dress in her budget.

The voices grew louder, and Lucy realized she was overhearing an argument.

"Absolutely not!" She recognized Phoebe's voice, sounding incredulous. "You've got to be kidding me, Camille. This is our opening weekend. We need all hands on deck."

"Oh, don't be so melodramatic," Camille scoffed. "The world's not going to end if I don't model your gowns for one event. I've already done the catalog shoot."

Phoebe's voice was firm. "This is not negotiable. You will be in attendance this weekend, or you can find another job."

Lucy winced, wishing she'd announced herself when she'd come in. She started inching toward the door, wondering if she should duck outside and come in again, this time making sure to call out a hello.

"You're going to fire me over this?" Camille sounded incredulous. "I'm your best model, Phoebe."

"That's exactly why I need you here this weekend," Phoebe retorted. "You can't just bail out at the last minute. It's not fair to the other girls, and it's not fair to me. If you're not going to be a team player, you should just quit now."

"I don't know who you think you are!" Camille sounded enraged. "But if you force my hand on this…"

Lucy froze as the voices seemed closer. They must be heading her way.

Phoebe's voice was deadly calm. "I'm done with your prima donna attitude, Camille. In or out. Make your decision."

The sound of heels clicking, and then Camille appeared in the corridor that led to the dressing room, seething with anger as she cast a final, bitter statement over her shoulder. "You're going to regret this, Phoebe. Mark my words."

On that ominous note, she stalked to the entrance, giving Lucy a withering look as she passed. The front door slammed behind her.

Lucy waited a few beats, shocked by what had just unfolded. She took a deep breath and called out, "Hello, Phoebe? It's me, Lucy Hale."

Phoebe instantly appeared, her face still flushed with anger. She gave Lucy an apologetic look as she came forward.

"I guess you heard all that," she waved a hand vaguely, reaching the sitting area and slumping into a chair wearily. She rubbed a hand over her face, looking distraught.

Lucy eased into a chair beside her. "Yes, I couldn't help but overhear. Sorry."

Phoebe shook her head. "That's just like Camille, to wait until the eleventh hour before making her demands. Always putting herself first."

Lucy was silent for a moment, not knowing how to respond. "Is it going to put you in a bind?"

Phoebe sighed, gazing moodily across the room. "We'll get through. It's going to make things a little tougher, but we can swing it. I'm used to having to pick up the pieces. Bad luck seems to follow me."

The last statement was so cryptic that Lucy couldn't help but think of how Phoebe had clammed up when Lucy had previously asked her about her past. It was on the tip of her tongue to press the woman now, but Phoebe suddenly straightened up, her eyes caught by the borrowed table.

"Oh, Lucy, thank you so much for lending me that table. I was afraid to ask Classic Fare if they had one. They probably would have charged me an arm and a leg."

Lucy frowned. "Surely, they would have lent it to you for free, seeing as you've chosen them to cater your event."

Phoebe gave a humorless laugh. "Let me tell you… Jackson Louis is nickel and diming me to death on this grand opening. I'll never use Classic Fare again."

Lucy was surprised. She'd always heard they had very competitive prices. "Hmm… really?"

Phoebe turned to meet her eyes, confiding, "I have a strong suspicion as to why that is. Mr. Louis has a grudge against me because I outbid him for this property. He was all set to expand his catering business, using this as a second location."

Lucy raised her eyebrows. "I didn't realize that."

Phoebe nodded. "You know, I wasn't aware that Jackson Louis and Classic Fare were linked, or I never would have chosen them for my caterer. All I knew about Classic Fare was that it's supposed to be very popular with the brides. I sure hope all this hassle is worth it."

Lucy assured her, "Oh, it will be. They have a very good reputation."

"Good," Phoebe remarked, though her spirits still seemed to be low. "Hopefully, this weekend's event will go off without a hitch. It's about time I had some good luck."

16

---

hoebe's words were still ringing in Lucy's ears as she made the drive home.

Her natural curiosity was piqued, but she didn't know Phoebe well enough to ask her pointed questions. Whatever bad luck had befallen the entrepreneur in the past, she hoped Ivy Creek would mark a new start. From what little conversation she'd had with Phoebe Pierce, she seemed to be a genuinely nice person, and Lucy wished her only the best.

Pulling into her driveway, Lucy closed her eyes briefly, fervently hoping she would not be confronted by another disaster zone, courtesy of the feuding felines. After the destruction of her bedroom, she'd left them to sort out their problems naturally, not shutting either cat away.

Crossing her fingers, she opened the door, scanning the living room. Neither cat was in sight. She tiptoed down the hall, wondering what they were up to.

Reaching her bedroom, Lucy saw Gigi lying stretched across the threshold, her gaze fixed on the shadowed area under the bed. She blinked at Lucy and rose, stretching languorously, and padded down the hall in the direction of the kitchen, a picture of innocence.

Lucy knelt down and peeked under the bed. Spooky's yellow eyes reflected back at her, wide with alarm.

Lucy sighed. The poor thing had probably been stuck under there all day. She decided the best course of action would be to put a small dish of food and water nearby. If that's where Spooky felt safe, she might be better off leaving her alone.

She rose to her feet and started down the hallway to find her aunt.

Aunt Tricia was sitting at the kitchen table, a cookbook open in front of her. The thick, hardcover tome had several scraps of paper bookmarking pages, and her aunt pored over a recipe, engrossed.

"Hi, Auntie," Lucy said, opening the fridge to grab a bottle of water. "What are you up to?"

Aunt Tricia glanced up distractedly. "Well, the effect of human hair as a deterrent did not last long. The deer have been in the garden again. Not that there was much to eat besides stumps of what they'd previously dined upon. I fear the summer squash will be next. They've run out of other options."

"Oh, no," Lucy sat down, dismayed. "I'm sorry." She knew how frustrated her aunt must be feeling by now.

Aunt Tricia waved her concern away. "I've made one last-ditch effort. I bought deer corn at the hardware store on the way home and piled it in the far corner of the yard as a decoy. But I'm no longer holding out hope for a prizewinning tomato crop this year. The deer have won on that front. And I've bought too many replacement flats already."

Lucy nodded, somewhat relieved they weren't about to try another crazy solution from the internet. She pointed at the book. "What are you looking up?"

"Squash recipes," her aunt responded, her voice brightening with enthusiasm. "With any luck, we'll have a bountiful harvest of summer squash, and it turns out there are a ton of ways to use them. Did you know you can actually make pickles from summer squash? And you can air fry them like French fries, too. You can even make noodles out of them, instead of pasta."

Lucy raised her eyebrows. *It was nice Aunt Tricia was conceding the war with the wildlife gracefully, but, personally; she wasn't too sure about the appeal of squash French fries.*

"Interesting," she said, rising from the table. "I guess I'm going to go change and take a shower."

Aunt Tricia nodded, already diving back into her cookbook. "Dinner's in an hour," she murmured, adding another bookmark.

The mention of food had Lucy's stomach grumbling. "Great! What are we having?"

"Summer squash stuffed with southwestern quinoa."

———

THE NEXT DAY at the bakery, Lucy filled Betsy and Hannah in on what she'd observed at Phoebe's bridal shop. Aunt Tricia had the day off. Lucy had heard her mention she was going to try out some new squash recipes.

"That Camille person should go back to where she came from," Betsy declared in disgust. "But I hope that will not affect the grand opening event too much."

"I doubt she's going anywhere," Lucy responded. "It looks like she and Dale Crane have become an item."

Hannah snorted. "Just like a man, to only care about the outside and be oblivious to the person underneath."

Betsy frowned. "That's quite a generalization. Joseph's not that way."

Lucy chimed in, "Neither is Taylor." She turned to ask Hannah. "Is Miles?"

"No…" Hannah admitted grudgingly. "But a lot of men are."

Lucy raised her brows. "As are a lot of women," she pointed out.

The bell chimed as a customer arrived, effectively halting the debate.

Lucy glanced up at the middle-aged man who'd entered.

He was wearing a gray suit, with a porkpie hat atop a head of salt and pepper hair. His slight paunch was straining at the buttons of his jacket, and he eyed the pastry case with interest.

"Good morning," Lucy greeted him, stepping forward. "Can I help you?"

He dragged his gaze from the chocolate eclairs with effort, an automatic smile coming to his lips. "May I speak to the owner, please?"

Lucy held out a hand, introducing herself. "You've found her. I'm Lucy Hale."

"Pleased to meet you," he said with a nod of respect. He fished a business card from his vest pocket and passed it to her. "Hal Buchman. I'm Vanna Verity's manager."

Lucy accepted the card, her smile in place, but her heart sank. *Was he here to place an order for Vanna's entourage?*

Although she still had some of their new product, Vanna's Vegan Carrot Cake Squares, in stock, Lucy didn't really relish devoting more time to a special, restricted-diet order today–they simply had too much to do.

"What can I help you with, Mr. Buchman?"

He rocked back on his heels, thumbs tucked into the front pockets of his slacks. "I'm sure you're aware my client is in town?"

Lucy nodded. "We're all planning to attend the grand opening at Phoebe's."

Betsy said from behind her, "I can't wait to meet her!"

Mr. Buchman nodded, pleased. "Well, Ms. Hale, I was hoping you'd agree to sell raffle tickets here at your bakery. The event itself will be pretty hectic, so I was thinking we'd let the good people of Ivy Creek buy their tickets ahead of time, and we'd only announce the winner at the grand opening. More streamlined process, you see."

Lucy was caught off guard. "A raffle? To benefit what, exactly?"

Mr. Buchman reddened slightly, nonplussed. "Ah… to help cover the travel expenses of Ms. Verity's gracious appearance at Phoebe's Bridal Shop." He hastened to add, "She's not being compensated by the town."

Lucy was silent for a moment, which spurred Mr. Buchman to elaborate.

"The tickets would only be a dollar each, and the winner would be awarded a photograph of themselves with Vanna Verity, taken by The Ivy Creek Ledger's photographer. The photo would be autographed, of course."

Lucy could almost hear Aunt Tricia's voice in her head. She cleared her throat. "And Sweet Delights Bakery? How would we benefit from that?"

Mr. Buchman frowned. "We would spread the word, of course, and you would conceivably get more foot traffic as people would come in to enter the raffle."

It was on the tip of Lucy's tongue to say no. The self-serving proposal, benefiting a celebrity as opposed to a charity, rubbed her the wrong way. And Mr. Hal Buchman seemed, in her opinion, a bit slippery himself.

But Lucy could feel Betsy's hopeful gaze upon her, and she reluctantly nodded her head. *The event was only a few days away, anyhow. It would be over and done with quickly.*

"OK," she accepted his proposal, and Mr. Buchman grinned hugely.

"Great! I'll just go and get the promotional material from my car, along with the raffle tickets. Thank you, Ms. Hale."

As Lucy watched the man eagerly dart outside to his vehicle, she reflected on the rumors bandied about town.

Was Vanna Verity's career going so badly that her manager needed to recoup their travel expenses?

Her curiosity about the celebrity was certainly rising. In just a few days, she'd meet Vanna in person.

17

"Oh, my goodness!" Betsy exclaimed from the back seat of Lucy's SUV. "I can't believe how many people have turned out for this!"

"Keep your eyes peeled for a parking space," Lucy instructed, slowing as she approached sixteen-hundred Main Street.

The much-awaited day of Phoebe's grand opening was upon them, and the crew had closed the bakery at noon, leaving themselves an hour to change clothes and meet at Lucy and Aunt Tricia's house. They had decided it was best for the four of them to take just one vehicle. And a good decision that had been, Lucy reflected, as it might take them a few minutes to find a single parking spot.

Main Street was bustling with women of all ages, and everyone seemed to have the same destination in mind. A line had formed outside the doors of Phoebe's Bridal Shop, waiting to be ushered inside.

"There's Mrs. White," Aunt Tricia pointed out from the front passenger seat. The regular customer of Sweet Delights was already standing in line, accompanied by her daughter and another teenage girl.

Lucy suspected the high turnout was, in part, due to the fact that Tate McQueen was slated to attend, and the young actor had quite a female fan base.

"There's one, Lucy!" Hannah announced from the backseat, pointing to a space in front of the hardware store being vacated by another driver.

Lucy immediately put on her directional, slowing to a stop as she waited. She watched in the rear-view mirror as the cars began to pile up behind her, with a few irritated drivers honking their horns in protest.

The other vehicle backed out, and Lucy quickly slipped into space with a sigh of relief. The competition for a close parking spot was brutal, but fortunately, they'd lucked out, and were only two doors down from Phoebe's.

The foursome piled out and began to walk briskly toward their destination, while Betsy chattered excitedly.

"This is my first time meeting a real celebrity," she commented, eyes shining. "Even if I don't manage to find the right dress, at least I'll have the memory of today." She turned to Hannah. "What do you think she'll be wearing?"

Hannah shook her head, amused. "Probably something that cost my entire year's salary."

They arrived at the back of the line just as the doors opened and the crowd began to surge forward.

"Stay together until we find our seats," Aunt Tricia advised, before turning to pin a censuring look on the eager young woman behind her who had jostled her. "Mind your elbows, please."

Lucy looked around the room as they stepped over the threshold. She was surprised that it looked larger than it had appeared during her earlier visit, despite the dozens of women squeezed into the space. There was a red-carpet runway rolled out from the dressing room area all the way to the back wall, and chairs had been arranged on either side. Tables were set up at the front of the room, bearing food, drink, and brochures advertising other wedding vendors. Lucy made a mental note to later ask Phoebe to carry some of the bakery's brochures.

"Lucy, hello!"

A familiar voice greeted her, and Lucy turned to see Phoebe, herself, wearing a pretty summer dress with gauzy bat-wing sleeves. Her face was flushed with excitement, her eyes sparkling as she was introduced to Aunt Tricia and Hannah.

"I've reserved four seats together for you guys," she said, leading the way. Turning to Betsy, she showed their seats, adding, "Here we are. You'll be close to where Vanna is sitting, and you'll have a great view of the runway."

Betsy smiled gratefully, touched that Phoebe had remembered her.

Their host's attention was suddenly caught by one of the models peeking out from the dressing room area. "I've got to go see how the girls are doing. I hope you all enjoy the show!"

Aunt Tricia sat down first, and Lucy, Hannah, and Betsy soon followed suit, watching as the attendees began to settle into chairs, one by one. When almost everyone had been seated, the doors opened again, and Mr. Hal Buchman walked in.

"My dear citizens of Ivy Creek," he began, holding up his hands for silence. A hush settled over the room as he announced, "Please welcome your Hometown Queen, the one and only Vanna Verity!"

A burst of applause sounded, and Vanna Verity strolled into the shop, on the arm of a handsome young man. Trailing behind her, Lucy recognized Debbie Ritner, whose face was filled with her usual anxious expression. A photographer followed the group, crouching in front of Vanna and snapping her picture from all angles.

Vanna was dressed in a caftan of royal purple, with her trademark platinum blond hair coiled up on her head in an elaborate style. Her face looked remarkably young for her age, which Lucy guessed to be in her late thirties. Her flawless complexion and wide cornflower blue eyes gave her the fresh-faced appearance of a woman a dozen years younger.

She faced the room, her lips curved into a practiced smile, waiting for the murmuring voices to stop. "Hello, ladies of Ivy Creek!" she greeted. "It's so good to be home!"

The crowd cheered and clapped, and several people, Betsy included, snapped the celebrity with their phones.

Vanna settled into her place of honor, a chair a few feet away from Lucy's group, as Hal Buchman instructed the crowd to quiet down.

"Let's all have a seat now, so Phoebe's show can begin. There will be time at the end of the event for picture taking."

While the rest of Vanna's entourage settled into the chairs around her, Debbie Ritner bent her head to listen to a whispered request from the star. Nodding her understanding, Debbie asked the townspeople sitting nearest Vanna to back up their chairs a few feet, giving the celebrity some space.

Slightly amused, Lucy instructed her own group to comply, noticing Aunt Tricia's expression had soured slightly. They settled in again, with Hannah sneaking peeks at Tate McQueen, who looked extremely bored as he lounged in his chair scrolling through his smart phone.

Hal Buchman was busy directing the photographer from The Ivy Creek Ledger, a patient man who seemed to take the manager's requests good-naturedly.

Lucy's eyes roamed the room, and her attention was suddenly caught by Phoebe, whose face seemed worried as she emerged from the dressing room area. Her harried expression had Lucy wondering if Camille's absence was creating problems for the other models.

Phoebe signaled for her assistant to close the drapes, and the shop's main lighting dimmed, leaving only the bright track lighting shining down on the runway.

The show was about to start.

18

---

*B*etsy watched, transfixed, as the models strutted down the red carpet one by one, stopping to pose at the end of the runway, turning this way and that so the gowns could be seen from all angles. Lucy observed that the other models were quite young, whereas Camille had appeared to be in her early thirties, although she obviously kept an eagle eye on her figure.

She glanced at Hannah, amused to see her friend was entertaining herself by watching the crowd, not really into the dresses at all. Aunt Tricia, however, seemed genuinely interested in the bridal gowns, leaning forward to view the third dress more closely. *She's probably envisioning how I'd look in that*, Lucy realized, chuckling to herself. Her aunt was clearly ready for Lucy and Taylor to tie the knot.

Lucy glanced over at Vanna curiously, and found the celebrity was having a whispered conversation with her fiancé, their heads bent close together. *Could it be that Vanna would actually purchase her wedding dress here, and not from some Hollywood designer?* For Phoebe's sake, Lucy sincerely hoped

104

so. She'd love to see another small business in Ivy Creek flourish.

The fourth gown was striking in its simplicity. Satin ivory, with tiny pearls accenting a modest scooped bodice, it was snug at the waist, flaring out at the hips. The floor-length skirt was gathered in the back, culminating in an elegant bow.

Betsy leaned forward with avid interest, murmuring, "Oh, I like that one." She consulted the program she'd retrieved from the brochure table, scanning down the list to see the price. Her face fell.

"How much is it?" Lucy whispered.

With a glum expression, her young friend answered. "Fifteen-hundred dollars."

Lucy's eyes widened. Although she didn't have a clue what wedding gowns cost, she thought that sounded a little high. And this gown looked even less elaborate than the others!

The show went on, and if there were any problems caused by Camille's absence, Lucy didn't detect them. She saw several women in the audience consulting their programs, and everyone seemed to be having a good time. After the twelfth gown was shown, the lights came back on, and the crowd applauded Phoebe, who came out from the back room looking pleased.

She thanked everyone for coming, adding that she'd be available for one-on-one consultations if anyone wanted to make an appointment.

"We'll have a short break, and then refreshments will be served." With a smile, Phoebe retreated to the back room once again.

Hal Buchman appeared in front of Lucy moments later. "Did you bring the raffle tickets?" he asked eagerly.

"I sure did," Lucy responded, pulling the large manilla envelope from her tote bag. She handed it over, adding, "Ninety-two entries."

Hal frowned. "Only ninety-two?" He peeked inside the envelope, containing cash and tickets. "Did you display the promo material I provided for you on the front counter?"

Lucy was stung by his attitude. She'd done the man a favor and he acted like she'd done him a disservice. "No, I set it on a small table with our vendors' products from Ivy Creek," she answered defensively. "But we did have a notice about it written on our daily special blackboard."

Hal looked irritated. "Well. Too late now. It is what it is." In a sarcastic tone, he added, "Thanks," before walking away.

Lucy shut her eyes briefly, striving to put the moment behind her. Something about that man really rubbed her the wrong way. But today was supposed to be a happy day for Betsy, so she wouldn't let Vanna's manager ruin it.

"Gee, when do you think they'll be serving the refreshments?" Hannah grumbled. "I'm famished."

As if on cue, there was a flurry of activity from the caterer's table, with Hal and the Ivy Creek Ledger's photographer conferring with a third man. Lucy suddenly recognized him from the picture on his website. It was Jackson Louis. She hadn't seen the owner of Classic Fare at the event until now and had assumed he wasn't present.

The photographer made his way to their side of the room, setting up for a shot of Vanna, just as Hal Buchman stepped to the center of the room, clearing his throat.

"Attention, please," he requested, and the low hum of chatter died down. He looked directly at Vanna Verity as he spoke.

"My dear Vanna… to show Ivy Creek's appreciation of your presence here today, the prestigious local catering outfit, Classic Fare, has created a special dessert just for you."

All eyes were on Vanna now, and her lips curved into a toothy smile. "What a sweet gesture," she remarked, punctuated with a tinkling laugh. "Pun intended, of course."

The crowd giggled at her joke, and Jackson Louis proceeded proudly across the room, bearing a tiny, covered, silver tray. The photographer lined up the shot, clicking away as the owner of Classic Fare unveiled his offering, whisking away the cover with a flourish.

From where Lucy sat, she had a clear view of the pink-glazed, star-shaped petit four, roughly six inches in diameter. Edible glitter had been sprinkled over the dessert, and Vanna's name was piped in icing across the top.

"Ms. Verity, I was honored to make this special dessert for you," Jackson said, flashing a smile at the celebrity. "And I want you to know, it's gluten-free, and vegan, as well as containing no refined sugar." He turned to face the camera as the flash went off, capturing the moment for The Ivy Creek Ledger.

"It was also intentionally made big enough for two," Jackson added, with a pointed look at Tate, who idly drummed his fingers on his knee, seeming to be a million miles away.

Vanna looked down at the cake, her eyebrows raised. "How delightful!" she exclaimed, accepting the tray. She turned her head this way and that, holding the plate up, posing as photos were snapped from around the room. "Thank you so much."

Debbie Ritner suddenly appeared at her elbow, offering her a napkin and fork.

Vanna's smile slipped slightly as she realized the photographer was waiting to snap a picture of her actually eating the dessert. She accepted the utensil, delicately cutting off a tiny corner of the cake.

Lucy watched, exchanging amused looks with Hannah as Vanna speared the morsel, balancing the fork near her mouth, lips parted slightly. Gazing straight at the camera, she waited, and Hal nudged the photographer to take his shot.

The flash went off, and Vanna set down her fork and plate at once, cake uneaten. She smiled warmly at Jackson, who looked a bit confused.

"I'm sure it's delicious," she assured him. "I'll have my assistant wrap it up so I can have it later in the afternoon when I need a pick-me-up."

Effectively dismissed, Jackson nodded graciously before turning away, heading to the buffet table to oversee the plating of petit fours for the rest of the attendees.

Her eyes still on Vanna, Lucy overheard the celebrity instruct Debbie in a low tone, as the assistant hovered at her elbow. "Take this away, please."

Debbie reached for the plate. "Wrap it for later?"

Vanna flicked her hand dismissively. "Good heavens, no. I have no desire to eat that. Who knows what qualifies for vegan or refined sugar around here." She shuddered theatrically.

19

*L*ucy heard Aunt Tricia huff out a breath, and realized her aunt had overheard the comment as well. *Vanna Verity was not as gracious as she appeared to be.* The realization hardened Lucy's heart a bit toward the "Hometown Queen".

A server appeared in front of Lucy's group, offering small plates of dessert, and Hannah accepted hers gladly. Betsy, Aunt Tricia, and Lucy followed suit.

"Coffee?" inquired another young woman, and Lucy nodded.

She took a bite of the small, vanilla glazed petit four on her plate, finding the dessert to be delicious. Jackson Louis had apparently taken her advice and had served the rest of the guests the traditional cake, saving the modified version for Vanna, alone.

"Oh, this is good," Betsy commented, turning to look at Lucy. "Not as good as yours, though."

Lucy smiled, privately agreeing. Her petit four recipe had been handed down through several generations of women in the Hale family, and in her opinion, it was top-notch. But Classic Fare's recipe was definitely a cut above the usual, though her practiced palate detected too much apricot glaze under the confectionary icing. The apricot glaze was meant to seal in moisture, she'd been taught, not compete with the cake and icing's flavor. Most people were not even aware of the glaze, if done right.

"Were you not listening? I said I wanted Perrier water." Vanna's displeased voice reached Lucy's ears. "I'm sure even a small town such as this has Perrier water!"

Lucy looked over to where Vanna was scolding Debbie Ritner, who looked miserable, wringing her hands.

"That is Perrier, Ms. Verity," she said timidly. "See the label?"

Vanna squinted at the label with a long-suffering sigh, handed the water back to her assistant.

"Well, it tastes unlike any Perrier I've ever had. Maybe it's expired. Does water expire?" She asked her entourage at large. Several of them shrugged, and the celebrity frowned, turning to her fiancé. "Tate. Does your Perrier taste funny?"

Tate appeared oblivious to the question, once again scrolling on his smart phone.

"Tate!" Vanna repeated crossly, bumping him with her knee.

The young man looked up, dragging his eyes from the screen. "What is it, Vanna?"

Vanna shook her head, disgusted by his inattentiveness. "Nothing. Forget it. Honestly, I don't know why you even joined me today."

She turned back to Debbie. "My special vitamin water is in the icebox compartment in the limo. Fetch that for me." She spotted the pink petit four Debbie had set aside, nearby. "And toss that in the trash, for heaven's sake. It makes me ill to look at it."

Chastised and red-faced, Debbie picked up the plated dessert and scurried away, her expression crestfallen.

Hannah leaned close to Lucy. "Hmm. The cat has claws," she murmured. "Maybe it's time for a nap."

Lucy agreed, but withheld comment. She watched as, across the room, Hal Buchman engaged the seated crowd one by one, apparently soliciting. She frowned, seeing him accept cash from one of the guests, passing out something in exchange. Squinting, she realized he was selling eight by ten-inch headshots of Vanna. *I guess the raffle didn't cover the travel expenses.*

Betsy seemed to be on the same wavelength, her thoughts turning to the drawing. "I wonder when they're holding the raffle?"

Hannah looked at her with a grin. "How many times did you enter?"

Betsy averted her eyes, confessing sheepishly, "Five."

Hannah hooted with laughter, and Aunt Tricia shushed her. "There's nothing wrong with that, Betsy. I hope you win."

Personally, having witnessed Vanna's less-than-kind treatment of Debbie, Lucy wasn't sure a photo op with the star was anything to treasure. Then again, she'd always had a soft spot for the underdogs.

"I'm sure they'll hold the raffle soon, Betsy." Lucy looked at her watch. "The event is supposed to be wrapping up any minute now."

Vanna's strident voice rang out behind her. "Where is that girl? Can't she do anything right? It's not like the limo is parked in the next state!"

Several pairs of eyes turned to look as Vanna's shrill tone carried across the room, summoning her manager.

"Hal!"

Hal looked up immediately, his hand stilling in the process of pocketing some bills.

"Hal!" Vanna waved him over impatiently.

The imperious command had the manager nearly tripping over his feet to cross the room quickly. Curiously, Lucy noted he seemed to be perspiring profusely, taking a handkerchief from his jacket pocket, and mopping at his shiny face.

"Yes, Vanna? Is something amiss?" Hal stood at Vanna's side, his head bent to her solicitously.

"Yes," responded Vanna in an icy tone. "No one in my employment seems to be doing their job today." She regarded the man with displeasure.

Hal blanched at her cross look. "Forgive me. What do you need?"

"My assistant! The girl that you hired," Vanna snapped. "I sent her out to get my special vitamin water from the limo and she never returned. For all I know, she ran off with some local yokel. I need you to find her, and if that proves difficult, then fire her. But most importantly, *bring me my vitamin water*."

The last bit was said through clenched teeth, and Hal hurriedly exited the room in search of Debbie. This time, Betsy had heard the entire conversation, and she stared at Vanna, her eyes round with shock and disillusionment.

Lucy's attention was distracted by Phoebe, bustling past her to reach Vanna's side, concerned there was a problem.

"Ms. Verity, is there anything I can get for you?" Phoebe's tone was smooth and professional, though there was no doubt she'd heard the lethal tone Vanna had used in dressing down Hal.

Vanna immediately switched on her trademark smile, accustomed to charming everyone she met.

"Oh, no, everything is lovely, Ms. Pierce. Thank you so much for having us."

Phoebe smiled graciously. "It was an honor to have you attend my grand opening, Ms. Verity." She glanced unobtrusively at her watch. "Will the raffle be taking place soon?"

Vanna's smile slipped slightly. "Yes, as soon as Mr. Buchman returns. He just ran out to fetch something from the limo."

"Excellent," Phoebe said, turning away.

At that moment, Hal rushed back into the shop, out of breath, his eyes wide with panic.

"Is there a doctor in the house? We need a doctor, quick!"

"What in the world?" Vanna stared at him, aghast.

Phoebe rushed to his side. "What is it? Are you ill?"

Hal shook his head, trying to catch his breath.

"It's not me, it's Debbie! She's collapsed!"

"I'm a nurse!" A woman called out from the far side of the room. She hurried forward, following Hal as he ran back outside.

Lucy, Hannah, Betsy, and Aunt Tricia rose as well, bolting for the doorway and spilling down the stairs and onto the sidewalk. The limo was parked right out front and the door to the back seat was wide open.

Lucy spotted Debbie Ritner's unconscious form slumped across the leather seat as the middle-aged nurse hurried to the opposite side of the car, yanking open the door.

"Oh, my goodness," breathed Betsy, a hand clutching her throat. "What could have happened?"

"Back up, people. Give her some room," Hal instructed. His face was pale as he waved the crowd back.

Intuitively, Lucy reached for her phone, ready to dial 911.

The nurse popped her head out from the car, her worried expression foretelling disaster.

"Call for an ambulance! I'm not getting a pulse. I'm going to start CPR."

"I'm calling 911 now," Lucy announced, punching the buttons and getting the emergency operator on the line. She spoke briskly into the phone, giving the address, and describing the situation. She was just hanging up when the nurse emerged from the limo, her expression somber.

"It's no use." The older woman's face was filled with sorrow as she looked from Hal to Phoebe.

"I'm afraid she's dead."

ead?" Lucy heard Vanna echo the nurse's words from where she stood near the doorway. "She can't be dead!"

The celebrity's tone was filled with disbelief. Hal immediately sprinted to her side.

"Vanna, let's get you back inside. You don't need to see this." He grabbed her elbow and steered her back into the shop.

"This is ridiculous. How can she be dead? She was fine, fifteen minutes ago." Vanna's voice faded away as she entered the building.

Lucy, Betsy, Hannah, and Aunt Tricia looked at each other, wide eyed and stunned by the turn of events.

"What do you think happened?" Betsy whispered, her lower lip trembling.

Lucy shook her head. "I don't know, Betsy. But we'll find out soon." She could hear the wail of the sirens as the first responders approached.

"Aunt Tricia, maybe you should take Betsy back inside. Get a drink of water. There's nothing to be done here." Lucy herself wanted to be there when the paramedics determined the cause of death, but she worried that Betsy was getting upset.

Aunt Tricia nodded, in a rare moment of speechlessness, and put an arm around Betsy's shoulder, leading the young woman back inside the shop.

As soon as they were out of earshot, Hannah stepped closer to Lucy, murmuring, "Do you think it was drugs?"

Lucy was shocked. "What? Why would you think that?" She hadn't got that sort of impression when she'd met Debbie.

Hannah shrugged. "It had to be something that killed her quickly. She's kind of young for a heart attack. And she always seemed jittery."

Lucy frowned and shook her head. "I think she was just nervous. Vanna doesn't seem like she would be an easy person to work for. And, besides, people of all ages have heart attacks. She might have had an undiagnosed condition."

Hannah nodded thoughtfully, agreeing, while her eyes scanned the street. "I wonder if anyone out here saw what happened."

A crowd of passersby had formed, gaping as the ambulance pulled up, followed by an Ivy Creek police cruiser. Lucy was relieved to see Taylor step out of the car, joined by another officer.

"Oh, good. Taylor's here. He should be able to tell us something."

Even as she spoke, Taylor looked up toward the shop, his face worried. Catching sight of Lucy and Hannah on the steps, his face cleared. He held up a finger for her to wait for him, and she nodded.

Hannah and Lucy watched as the paramedics carefully lifted Debbie's body from the limo onto a stretcher, checking her vital signs. A moment later they were shaking their heads, slowly covering her with a sheet.

Taylor's rangy form was bent over inside the limo, inspecting the interior. He straightened and walked over to one of the paramedics, briefly conferring with him, before turning to his fellow officer, issuing instructions. The policeman nodded, retrieving an evidence bag from the cruiser, and ducking inside the limo.

Lucy's gaze was fixed on Taylor's face as he climbed the steps to join her. He appeared very concerned, taking hold of her forearms and peering anxiously into her face.

"Are you OK?" he asked, before glancing at Hannah. "Both of you?"

Lucy was puzzled. She nodded. "We're fine. What do you think happened?"

Taylor's voice was grim. "We won't know for sure until the coroner performs an autopsy, but from my initial take on the scene, I'd guess it was a case of poisoning."

Hannah and Lucy gasped as one.

"Poison?" Lucy echoed, her eyes wide. "From... what?"

Taylor's blue eyes looked worried. "There's no way to know for sure until the contents of her stomach are analyzed. But we did find an empty tray with sticky pink glaze and glitter on the seat beside her, and a fork in the footwell."

His brows drew together as he posed an urgent question. "Is that something everyone ate during the show?"

Lucy's mind spun, processing the information. *Debbie must have eaten the special petit four made for Vanna, instead of tossing it in the trash as instructed. And now she was dead...*

"Lucy." Taylor's voice broke through her thoughts. "Hannah. Did everyone eat the same thing? Did you two eat something with pink icing? Or Betsy, or Tricia?"

Lucy shook her head as Hannah chimed in. "No, that was a dessert made specifically for Vanna. Debbie was supposed to throw it away when Vanna didn't want it."

Lucy nodded in confirmation, still speechless. Taylor took a notepad from his jacket.

"I need some information, starting with the victim's name."

Lucy answered his questions on autopilot, still numb from the news. She didn't know a lot of details about Debbie and told Taylor that Hal Buchman, Vanna's manager, was inside. He would know more.

Taylor nodded, tucking his notebook away. "I'll go talk to him. Are you OK to drive, Lucy?"

She nodded her head.

Taylor dropped a kiss on her forehead. "Good. I want you ladies to go on home. If anyone feels in the least bit unwell, go immediately to the hospital. I'll let you know once we have an official cause of death."

Lucy took a deep breath, following Taylor into the building to collect Aunt Tricia and Betsy.

She struggled to make sense of the news. *Had Debbie eaten something earlier that was toxic? Or had Vanna's petit four been a deadly dessert?*

———

IT WAS mid-morning the next day before Taylor had any news. Lucy listened, feeling a chill run down her spine, with the bakery's phone clutched tightly to her ear as he relayed the findings. She hung up the phone and turned to face Hannah, Betsy, and Aunt Tricia, where they'd gathered beside her.

"It was poison," she confirmed, still numb with disbelief. "Debbie died from poisoning. The coroner says the only thing in her stomach was the pink petit four cake."

"Oh, my goodness," Aunt Tricia looked stricken. "Could it have been an accident? Botulism or some sort of pathogen like that?"

Hannah gripped the counter for support. "Are they sure the rest of the cakes were OK?"

Lucy nodded. "Taylor said they analyzed the regular petit fours left at the scene, and they were all fine. Apparently, it was something in Vanna's specialty cake, only."

Betsy's eyes widened. "Does that mean someone was trying to kill Vanna Verity?" Her voice came out as a squeak at the end.

Lucy took a deep breath, releasing it slowly. So many thoughts were running through her head. "I don't know,

Betsy. It's starting to look that way. Taylor says it was not a naturally occurring pathogen, so it's hard to believe it was an accident."

"What happens now?" Aunt Tricia asked. "Do they have a suspect?"

Lucy relayed Taylor's words. "They're going to search Classic Fare, first. Taylor's also running a background check on everyone in Vanna's entourage."

The four women grew silent, each thinking of Debbie Ritner, and how hard she'd tried to please her boss.

The one directive Debbie had decided to ignore—to throw away the pink petit four—had ultimately resulted in her death.

21

*L*ucy lay on the couch in her living room the next evening, trying to interest herself in a new novel. She'd felt jittery since the day of the murder, stunned by how close she and her tight-knit group had come to eating a poisoned sweet.

It could have been any one of us, she thought. *Until we find out exactly what happened, we don't know a thing. It wasn't necessarily a targeted poisoning. It could have been a plan to poison hundreds, or even thousands of people, by some random sicko tampering with ingredients.*

She remembered when she was a child, there had been a scare with poisoned over-the-counter pain relievers, leading to the safety seals on today's bottles. There were crazy people out there, willing to kill innocent strangers, just for their own sick gratification.

With that horrific thought on her mind, she rose from the couch, laying the book down, and got out her laptop. She punched 'poisoned bakery ingredients' into a Google search box and waited for the results to pop. She tried to quash the niggling worry in the back of her mind that perhaps her own stores of almond flour or coconut sugar at Sweet Delights could be contaminated.

For the next several minutes, she engrossed herself in stories of poisonings of baked goods occurring in the early nineteen-hundreds, but could find no cases relevant to today. She shut down the laptop, still worrying, just as the telephone rang.

It was Taylor.

"Hey, sweetheart," his warm voice greeted her, and she felt better immediately. "How was work today?"

Lucy relayed how the town had begun to buzz with gossip about the murder, the regular customers lingering over coffee and pastries as everyone swapped theories on what had actually happened.

"Are you planning to make a statement soon?" Lucy was troubled by the misinformation floating around. "People are looking for someone to blame, and pretty soon they'll be pointing fingers at either Classic Fare or Phoebe Pierce."

Personally, Lucy hoped the poisoning proved to be a random crime, not attached to anyone in Ivy Creek.

Taylor sounded pensive. "At this point, there's not much we can tell the citizens to allay their fears," he confessed. "We searched Classic Fare, and analyzed the ingredients used in making Vanna's cake, but nothing popped. We even analyzed the contents of their dumpster."

"Where did you get the list of ingredients?" Lucy asked. "The petit four's ingredients weren't the usual ones you'd expect. Mr. Louis had to make several modifications."

Taylor assured her, "Yes, Mr. Louis provided us with your emailed recipe for Vanna's vegan, gluten-free, no refined sugar version, and we went through those ingredients one by one."

"And nothing? No contaminants?" Lucy wasn't sure if this was good news or bad news. She'd feel better if they knew exactly how the cake had been poisoned. "Did you check the edible glitter? And the pink food coloring?" Those items would not have been on her list, but she knew they'd been used to make Vanna's star-shaped cake.

"Yes," Taylor replied. "We might have missed checking those, but Mr. Louis was the one to bring it to our attention, and we tested those bottles, as well."

Lucy frowned, beginning to get frustrated. "If the poisoning wasn't in any of the ingredients at Classic Fare's kitchen, how did it get into the cake?"

Taylor was silent for a moment. "It's possible the poison was added to Vanna's cake on site, at the bridal shop. Maybe a syringe or eyedropper was used after the dessert was already plated."

Lucy thought that scenario over. "So, anyone who was in attendance, who had access to the dessert, could have poisoned it."

Taylor agreed. "Exactly. Do you remember where the food was kept before it was served? Was it in plain sight? Or in the back? Was anyone hovering nearby?"

"It was in plain sight," Lucy replied immediately, picturing the buffet table. "But no one would have thought twice about seeing one of the catering crew fussing with the desserts. That's kind of what they do."

She had a sudden thought. "You know, Phoebe told me that Jackson Louis had a grudge against her. Apparently, he'd bid on the same property with an eye toward expanding his catering business. She said he was pretty bitter that she'd outbid him. Is it possible this could all be an attempt to drive Phoebe's business into the ground? If she closed up shop, Mr. Louis would probably benefit." She felt slightly guilty for raising suspicion against the man, but she and Taylor were just tossing ideas back and forth.

Taylor made a noncommittal sound. "Anything's possible, but I don't think so. He'd be shooting himself in the foot. I mean, even now, I'm sure people are wondering how safe it is to have Classic Fare cater their events. Even though we didn't find any evidence in their kitchen, this will stick in the minds of the townspeople. No doubt his business will suffer."

While Lucy pondered his words, Taylor spoke again, with a pointed question. "How about Hal Buchman, Lucy? Do you remember seeing him near the food?"

Lucy closed her eyes, thinking. "Well, I guess so. He was pretty much all over the room, directing the photographer from the newspaper, talking to the catering crew, moving chairs around."

She reflected on her impressions of the man. A little desperate, maybe even shady.

"Do you have reason to suspect Hal?"

Taylor took a moment before answering. "Let's just say he's the one I'm focusing on at the moment. I did some poking around and found out he took a big life insurance policy out on Vanna two years ago. But that's not a crime. And it's not even unusual for a manager of a celebrity to do that–

completely justifiable, in fact, as the star is their main source of income."

Lucy got goosebumps, hearing Taylor's words.

"How big of a life insurance policy are we talking about?"

Taylor's reply stunned her.

"One million dollars."

---

22

*A*unt Tricia popped into the kitchen where Lucy and Hannah were busy replenishing the morning supplies of pastries.

Business had been up since the murder, as Sweet Delights had become a hub for conversation. Tables were filled with customers who normally took their orders to go, but now wanted to stay and chatter excitedly about how Vanna Verity had narrowly escaped death.

It was only eleven in the morning, and nearly all the tables in the front room were filled, and the veranda upstairs was filling up fast.

"Do we have anymore apple turnovers?" she asked. "Mrs. White just bought us out."

Lucy shook her head. "We ran out of apple filling, but there are blueberry turnovers in the oven." She finished de-panning a coffee cake, expertly cutting it into uniform squares, and setting the pieces in paper liners.

"What does Mrs. White have to say about the murder?" inquired Hannah, filled with curiosity. She piped zig-zagging lines of glaze over a tray of cherry scones and passed it to Aunt Tricia.

Aunt Tricia pursed her lips. "Well, the most interesting thing she said was that Phoebe's Bridal Shop has just extended their hours. Oddly enough, their popularity has gone through the roof in the last few days, with everyone wanting to take a look at where Vanna Verity was nearly murdered."

"Rather morbid," Lucy commented. "But not surprising."

Hannah agreed, as Aunt Tricia turned away, heading back to the front counter with the scones.

"People do seem to have a thing for visiting scenes with a tragic history. You see it all the time on TV. Crowds lining up to take tours where mass murders occurred, or a famous person was shot."

Lucy shook her head as she took the dirty pan over to the industrial sink. "I never understood that fascination. But I have to say, I'm pleased that Phoebe's business was not destroyed as a result of what happened. I really like her. I'm looking forward to doing business with her in the future."

"Has Taylor said if they have any leads?"

Lucy responded over her shoulder while she scrubbed the coffee cake pan. "Well, Classic Fare has been searched, and there was no sign of the poison there. Just between you and me, Taylor was taking a hard look at Hal Buchman, Vanna's manager. Apparently, he'd taken out a large life insurance policy on Vanna."

Hannah raised her eyebrows, commenting, "Money is very often the motive for murder…"

Lucy agreed, drying her hands on a dish towel. She walked over to the oven to peek inside at the turnovers. *A light golden brown, but no sign of filling bubbling at the seams yet... another ten minutes.* She set the timer, continuing their conversation.

"The problem is, he can't figure out when Mr. Buchman would have had access to the dessert. If you remember, the silver tray holding Vanna's petit four was covered, and no one Taylor has questioned reports seeing Mr. Buchman ever lifting the cover."

Lucy knew Taylor had been frustrated by this dead-end, after he'd questioned several of Classic Fare's servers. Everyone had said the same thing. No one had witnessed anyone removing the silver tray's cover except for Jackson Louis.

Reportedly, the owner of Classic Fare had inspected all the desserts upon his late arrival at the bridal shop, making sure everything was perfect before the food was served.

This bit of information only added to Lucy's original suspicions. Jackson Louis had wanted that location on Main Street. If he knew the police wouldn't find any evidence at his catering business, then he may have assumed Classic Fare's reputation would not be tarnished. The police might chalk it up to a random contamination of bulk ingredients, with no particular target. And if Phoebe's Bridal Shop went under, then he'd have his wish.

It would have been easy enough for the man to discreetly add poison to the cake, using an eyedropper from a vial hidden in his pocket, she speculated. *He was a rather large man. He could have shielded his actions from view simply by turning his back to the crowd. It would have only taken a second. By poisoning the cake on site, he would have ensured that the kitchens at Classic Fare would hold no trace of his actions.*

Jackson Louis was the foremost suspect in Lucy's mind. As she began to mix a batch of devil's food cake batter, she wondered how she might convince Taylor to take a second look at the man.

———

THAT AFTERNOON, as Lucy was filing invoices upstairs in the bakery's office, she was surprised by a knock on the doorframe.

Turning, she was happily surprised to see Taylor. "Well, hello there!" She crossed the room and gave him a peck on the cheek. "Stopping by for a late lunch?"

Taylor shook his head. "No, I wanted to ask you something." He pointed at the chairs. "Do you have a minute?"

Lucy nodded, sitting behind the desk, as Taylor lowered himself into the leather chair opposite her.

"What's up?"

Taylor steepled his fingers, gathering his thoughts. "Didn't you tell me that Phoebe had stopped by the bakery to introduce herself?"

Lucy nodded. "Yes, a few days before the grand opening. She was talking about putting together package deals for brides-to-be, including the dress, the cake, and the flowers. Why do you ask?"

Taylor met her eyes with a serious gaze. "Did she mention where she'd relocated from?"

The hairs on the back of Lucy's neck began to prickle. She remembered how Phoebe had brushed off her questions that afternoon, in a most curious manner.

"No," she replied slowly, hating the idea of Phoebe as a suspect in the murder. *Clearly, that's where this was going.*

She sighed, confessing, "To be honest, I asked her directly, and she didn't answer me. It seemed to make her uncomfortable, and she left almost immediately afterward." Her face troubled, she asked him, "Why do you want to know?"

Taylor's expression was grim. "I ran her name through records just as a matter of course. Nothing popped up, not a single thing. So, I got a copy of her business license from the town hall and ran her EIN. It doesn't match."

Confused, Lucy leaned forward, questioning him. "What do you mean, it doesn't match?"

Taylor's tone was flat as he elaborated.

"Phoebe Pierce doesn't exist. The woman running Phoebe's Bridal Shop is using an assumed name."

23

*L*ucy's mouth dropped open in shock. "What? What does that mean?"

Taylor's tone was measured. "It only means that I need to find out why."

Lucy frowned, her mind spinning. "But… isn't that illegal?"

Taylor shook his head. "As long as her legal name is on all relevant paperwork with the state and federal governments, she can call herself anything she'd like. It raises questions, though. I need to know why. Most people change their name because they're running from something in their past. Since a murder just occurred at her new place of business, I have to make sure there haven't been other instances of foul play in her past."

Lucy remained pensive, sorting through it all. "Does that mean she's a suspect?"

Taylor sighed. "I would say I'm not ruling her out. I need to go ask her some questions. Some women use an assumed name when they're trying to escape from an abusive situation. Possibly, that's the case, here."

Lucy drummed her fingers on the desk, thinking. Personally, she hoped Phoebe could give Taylor a valid reason for not using her legal name. If the woman was out to make a fresh start, through no fault of her own, Lucy already felt sympathetic toward her. Add to that, a murder happening just as she'd set up shop... perhaps bad luck really was following her, just as she'd mentioned to Lucy. In her heart, Lucy didn't feel the woman she'd met was capable of violence.

"I had planned to just pop in to chat with her this afternoon," Taylor said. "But when I drove by her shop, it looked pretty busy."

Lucy nodded. "Mrs. White said Phoebe had to expand her hours to keep up with the requests for appointments. I guess everyone in town wants to see where Vanna Verity was almost murdered." She shuddered. "I never knew the citizens of Ivy Creek were so morbid."

Taylor narrowed his eyes. "Hmm. Interesting how a murder on their opening weekend skyrocketed the shop's popularity."

Lucy bit her lip, wishing she hadn't said anything. It sounded like she'd just given Taylor another reason to suspect Phoebe.

Taylor stood, stretching. "I need to get back to work."

Lucy rose, standing on her tiptoes to kiss his cheek. "You should come by the house when you can. We have mountains of summer squash."

"Any tomatoes?" Taylor asked hopefully, turning to the doorway.

Lucy smiled ruefully. "Not this year. The deer and rabbits have won the battle of the garden. We're lucky they don't seem to like summer squash."

"Go figure…" Taylor mumbled, heading for the stairs.

———

WHEN LUCY ARRIVED home that evening, after catching up on her bookkeeping, she found Aunt Tricia in the kitchen, surrounded by a mountain of summer squash in every form imaginable. There was a platter of thinly sliced, golden brown, squash "chips" set in front of the air fryer, a delicious-smelling, cheesy, squash casserole was cooling on the counter, and her aunt was busy quartering yet more summer squash, while a deep pot of boiling water simmered on the stove, sterilizing pickling jars.

Lucy's hand hovered above the squash chips. "Are these for us?"

"Yes," Aunt Tricia replied before indicating the squash casserole with a jut of her chin. "But that one's for Chloe Barnes, so don't poke at it."

Lucy nodded, plucking a still hot squash chip from the top of the pile and crunching down on it. It was surprisingly good.

"And what are you making there?" she inquired, watching as Aunt Tricia capped another slender yellow squash.

"Squash pickles," Aunt Tricia replied with a sideways glance.

The answer didn't surprise her, but the presence of two new boxes of pickling jars stacked on the kitchen table did raise a new question.

Lucy cocked her head. "How many are you making?" Each box held a dozen jars, and she knew her aunt had several jars left over from last year's dill pickle season.

Aunt Tricia set down her knife, turning to the stove and stirring a brine mixture. "By my calculations, today's batch will yield nineteen jars… but there will be more squash ready to go by tomorrow. I'm trying to find the least perishable way of using up our summer squash."

She turned to regard Lucy over the top of her glasses. "Feel free to make a gift of as many jars as you can."

Lucy chuckled, crunching another squash chip. "I'll do that." She had a sudden thought. "In fact, I may bring a jar over to Phoebe Pierce tomorrow. I was thinking of stopping by her shop."

"Oh?" Aunt Tricia turned, giving Lucy her full attention. "Did you see a dress you liked at the show?"

Lucy shook her head, amused by her aunt's thought process. "No, Auntie, I'm far from ready to choose a wedding gown. But I did want to chat with Phoebe a bit."

Her conversation with Taylor earlier that day had filled Lucy with purpose. If Phoebe was running from an unfortunate incident in her past, she wanted to offer her support. Bringing by a jar or two of squash pickles would provide an unusual, but useful, icebreaker.

Her aunt narrowed her eyes before turning back to her cutting board and lining up another yellow squash to be quartered.

"I hope you're not planning to solve this murder yourself." Her aunt's tone was censuring as she transferred the squash quarters to a bowl. "You know Taylor doesn't appreciate you stepping on his toes."

Guilt pricked at Lucy's conscience. Although her main reason to visit Phoebe was to satisfy her own curiosity about the woman using an assumed name - while offering what support she could give - she had the idea that Phoebe may have witnessed something important before the murder and perhaps did not even realize it. A few questions wouldn't hurt anything… and Taylor wouldn't even have to know.

"I have the utmost faith in Taylor's abilities, Auntie, you know that," Lucy answered evasively, then changed the subject.

"Where's Gigi? Or Spooky, for that matter?" Her Persian always greeted her at the door, and she'd yet to make an appearance.

Aunt Tricia sighed. "Gigi has decided that Spooky is not allowed out from under the bed. The poor thing wandered in here about an hour ago, and Gigi was quick to chase her back to the bedroom. I assume that's where they still are, jailor and prisoner."

Lucy shook her head silently, going to the cabinet to retrieve two cat treats. It was a shame that Gigi was so inhospitable, but Spooky would only have to put up with being an unwanted guest for a little while longer.

24

*L*ucy drove through town the next morning, on her way to Phoebe's Bridal Shop. On the front passenger seat lay two jars of squash pickles, as well as three photos of wedding cakes for Phoebe to use for promotion in her package deal for brides.

She'd called Phoebe first thing this morning, intending to leave a message, and was surprised when the woman answered, at half past seven. Phoebe had told her she'd been so swamped with appointments that she'd needed to come in early to organize after a late appointment last night. She invited Lucy to come by before the shop officially opened at nine.

As Lucy drove past Crane's Formal Wear, she was struck by the large banner the business had put up, stretching from end to end of the plate-glass window.

Everything on Sale – 50% - 70% Off!

She raised an eyebrow, surprised. In all the years she'd lived in Ivy Creek, she'd never seen Crane's hold such a huge sale, nor advertise so desperately. It made her wonder if Crane's Formal Wear was already suffering from their new competition.

Minutes later, Lucy was pulling into a parking space in front of Phoebe's. She gathered up her items from the passenger seat, checking her watch. She only planned to spend a few minutes talking to the other shop owner and crossed her fingers it would be a productive visit.

"Hello, Lucy!" Phoebe greeted her as she walked in the door.

The other woman was wearing a lovely summer dress in peacock blue with a gathered skirt. Her eyes were bright and sparkling as Lucy set her gift of squash pickles on the counter.

"Oh, the squash pickles!" she exclaimed. "I can't wait to try them. I'd never heard of making pickles from anything but cucumbers."

"My Aunt Tricia is a big fan of the old adage: *waste not, want not*," Lucy quipped. "Now that the deer and rabbits have eaten all our other vegetables, it's squash everything. You'd be amazed with the dishes she's come up with."

Phoebe chuckled, leading the way over to a pair of oversized blue chairs. "Coffee?"

Lucy accepted a cup, settling in. She was wondering how to broach the subject that had been on her mind when Phoebe beat her to the punch.

"Lucy, I've heard that you and the deputy sheriff are a romantic couple," she began, meeting Lucy's eyes. At Lucy's surprised expression, she continued. "I'd like to clear something up, if you don't mind."

Phoebe took a sip of her coffee and set the cup down, folding her hands primly in her lap. "Taylor came to visit me yesterday with some questions about the name I'm using. I'm not sure if he had shared his findings with you…?"

Flushing slightly, Lucy nodded. "He did say there was a mismatch… with the name on your EIN." She felt slightly uncomfortable, but figured the best way to get answers was to be upfront.

Phoebe looked pensive for a moment, then locked her gaze on Lucy's, her blue eyes guileless.

"I believe I'd mentioned to you that bad luck seems to follow me. One of the darkest periods in my life was when I lived in Philadelphia for twelve years. My ex-husband…" She trailed off for a moment, looking stricken.

"It's OK, Phoebe," Lucy assured her, gently. "You don't have to go into the details. I assume you needed to get away from a bad situation?"

The other woman looked grateful. "Yes. That's exactly why I picked up and left. Things were out of control, and I began to fear for my safety. Ivy Creek was meant to be a fresh start, and I didn't think I could accomplish that with my former name."

When Lucy looked up curiously at her wording, Phoebe clarified. "For all intents and purposes, I *am* Phoebe Pierce now. I'm currently petitioning the court for a legal name change."

Lucy nodded, feeling better about the situation. She reached over and squeezed the other woman's hand. "If there's anything you need, please don't hesitate to ask."

Phoebe smiled. "Thank you." She seemed to hesitate for a moment before venturing, "Lucy? You don't think Taylor will... I mean, I'd like to keep that information private. God knows the Cranes would use it to their advantage if they knew."

Lucy frowned. "The Cranes? As in Crane's Formal Wear?" She thought about the banner she'd seen. "Are they giving you a hard time?"

Phoebe sighed. "When I first opened up shop, the father and son came to see me. They wanted to collaborate and suggested we make Phoebe's Bridal Shop an extension of Crane's Formal Wear. They argued that I'd have an easier time if I agreed to do that, as their reputation in this town is solid. But I really wanted to make something *for* myself, *by* myself, without anyone's help. So, I politely refused their offer."

"What happened then?" Lucy asked, not liking at all how this sounded. To her ears it appeared that Peter and Dale Crane had tried to pressure Phoebe, in order to save their own business from floundering under the weight of competition.

Phoebe shrugged. "They weren't happy, but there was nothing they could do about it. I was actually kind of nervous when I found out Dale worked as a chef at Classic Fare, but at that point I'd already hired them to cater the event."

She leaned forward conspiratorially. "Although Dale wasn't here on the day of the grand opening, I did mention to

Taylor that he might look into Dale's involvement with the food preparations that day."

Lucy was stunned at the implication. "Do you really think Dale could have been involved in the poisoning?"

Phoebe looked troubled. "I'd like to say no, but... someone poisoned that cake, Lucy. I don't want to point any fingers, but I thought Taylor should be aware of the history."

Lucy's mind spun. Even though Classic Fare had been searched, and there had been no trace of the poison on the premises, if the Cranes *were* involved, there might be evidence either at the tuxedo shop, or even at Peter or Dale Crane's homes.

It seemed like a pretty big leap, that the murder could have been committed over a business trying to eliminate their competitor, but what Phoebe had pointed out was true.

Someone had poisoned the cake for their own nefarious reasons.

One thing was certain.

Lucy needed to talk to Taylor.

25

Lucy hung up her cell phone after leaving Taylor a message to call her. She stared into space for a moment, turning over the possibilities in her mind. *Dale Crane had seemed like such a nice young man. Would he really have resorted to murder to protect his family's business?*

It seemed farfetched. Perhaps she was missing something.

Lucy started the car and made the drive across town to the bakery, arriving just after Aunt Tricia. The older woman was just getting out of her car, loaded down with an armful of yellow summer squash.

Amused, Lucy rescued her aunt's purse, which was dangling precariously from two fingers.

"Thank you," Aunt Tricia said, following Lucy as she unlocked and opened the door. She went directly to the front counter and unburdened herself, catching an errant squash as it rolled off the edge.

"What's with all the squash?" Lucy asked, eyeing the vegetables suspiciously. "Please tell me you didn't find a recipe online for squash cupcakes."

Aunt Tricia narrowed her eyes, trying to tell if Lucy was joking. "I just thought I'd give a few squash out to some of our regular customers," she explained.

Lucy raised her eyebrows, waiting, and Aunt Tricia confessed. "Well, I saw a variation of zucchini bread that uses yellow squash, so I thought I might give it a try."

Lucy shook her head, chuckling, as the door opened and Betsy came in next.

"What was I thinking?" Betsy complained, her usual cheery face looking grumpy and out-of-sorts. "There's got to be a way for Joseph and me to have the wedding we want. My mother is driving me crazy!"

She set her purse down on the front counter. "What's going on here?" She looked puzzled, showing the squash.

"You can take some home, if you like," Aunt Tricia offered immediately. "They're quite versatile."

"Hmm," Betsy picked one up, admiring it. "OK, thanks. I'll add it to a stir-fry tonight."

"Here, have another," Aunt Tricia said, passing her a second one.

The sound of the back door closing carried to the front, and they all turned expectantly. Hannah emerged a minute later, coming through the kitchen archway.

"Good morning, all," she greeted. She zeroed in on Aunt Tricia right away.

"You know that tip you gave me about a tomato juice bath to take out the skunk stink?"

Aunt Tricia nodded. "Did it work?"

Hannah offered a wry smile. "Only after three baths in the stuff. Then it did. But now I have another problem."

"What's that, dear?" Aunt Tricia asked, picking up a squash and handing it to her. Hannah accepted it, looking down at it, bemused, before glancing up at Tricia quizzically. "You should try some summer squash chips in your air fryer, Hannah. Very delightful."

Hannah blinked and set the squash down. "Thanks. My problem is Sampson. He doesn't smell bad anymore, no, no... although the same can't be said for my apartment. But now, Sampson is... pink. He's a pink shepherd, as opposed to a white shepherd."

All three women looked at Hannah with identical puzzled expressions.

"Pink? Like, *pink*, *pink*?" asked Betsy.

Hannah nodded glumly. "As pink as bubble-gum. I guess white shepherds shouldn't be bathed in tomato juice. At least, not three times in a row."

Lucy couldn't help but laugh, and soon Betsy giggled as well, envisioning Miles's large, pink dog. Aunt Tricia's lips twitched, but she kept it under control.

"Have you bathed him in regular shampoo?"

Hannah nodded. "Nothing's working."

Aunt Tricia handed her another squash. "It will probably wear off in time," she mused. "At least, I think it will..."

Hannah's shoulders slumped. "I sure hope it wears off before Miles comes back."

————

THE WORKDAY WAS SOON UNDERWAY, but even as Lucy busied herself with baking, decorating, and chatting with customers, Phoebe's words replayed in her mind. It wasn't until a young couple had seated themselves at one of the bistro tables, cozying up, lost in each other's eyes, that Lucy suddenly was struck by a memory.

Dale and Camille tucked away at a corner table, having a romantic dinner at McIntyre's Steakhouse.

Her eyes widened. Dale was so smitten with Camille, he had been willing to do anything to get Camille to date him. He was already resentful that Phoebe's Bridal Shop might be the downfall of his family's business. And Camille had been fired by Phoebe.

Could the model have played on that and elicited Dale's help in her own twisted need for revenge?

The memory of Camille's angry face as she stalked out of Phoebe's shop replayed itself in Lucy's mind. She could almost hear Camille's bitter words, tossed over her shoulder.

"You're going to regret this, Phoebe. Mark my words."

Lucy jolted herself out of her reverie. "I'll be right back," she said to Betsy, heading for her office.

Taylor had not called her back yet. As much as she didn't want to bother him, she felt compelled to share her revelation. She dialed his number, relieved when he picked up on the second ring.

"Taylor, hey. It's me." Lucy could hear a lot of commotion in the background. "Can you hear me?"

A muffled reply, and a moment later Taylor spoke again, his voice clearer, but harried.

"Hi, Lucy. I got your message, but we've had quite a morning. Tim Brisbane caught Don Good's German shepherd breaking into his henhouse and fired a round in the air to scare him off. Now both men are in here, mad as heck at each other."

Lucy shut her eyes, wishing she were there in person, so she could have his full attention.

"Taylor, I talked to Phoebe this morning, and she told me about the Cranes' visit when she first got to town. Are you looking at Dale Crane as a suspect in the poisoning?"

Taylor put a hand over the mouthpiece to reply to someone else before answering.

"I can't really see either Dale or Peter Crane resorting to murder, Lucy. They were just trying to make a business deal with Phoebe."

Lucy frowned. "But Taylor, do you remember seeing Dale Crane with that model, Camille, when we were at McIntyre's? Camille had just been fired from Phoebe's, and when I was there, I overheard her saying–"

Taylor interrupted her, his voice firm. "I've really got to get back to work, Lucy. Can we talk about this later?"

Lucy huffed out a breath. "But I heard Camille–"

"Lucy. I've got to go, I'm sorry. I promise I'll call you back when things settle down."

The line clicked, and Lucy stared down at the phone, frustrated. She shook her head, annoyed, realizing there was nothing she could do but wait.

Descending the staircase a moment later, her mind miles away, she bumped straight into a young woman who was leaving the bakery. The woman's iced coffee was jostled by Lucy's elbow, the lid coming loose, and the beverage splashed across the sleeve of the young woman's blouse.

"I'm so sorry!" Lucy exclaimed, embarrassed. She looked at the other woman's face, thinking she looked familiar. "Here, let me help. We don't want that to stain."

Lucy quickly steered her over to the sink behind the bakery's front counter.

"Oh, you don't need to fuss," the customer assured her. "It's not a big deal."

Lucy produced a bottle of club soda and a rag from under the cabinet. "This will just take a second…"

She dabbed at the woman's sleeve, then peeked curiously up at her face. "Have we met?"

The young woman smiled. "Not formally, but I saw you at the bridal show. I'm Aimee, one of Phoebe's models."

"Ah," Lucy replied, nodding. "Yes, that must be it." She added, "You guys did a great job, even though you were down a model."

When Aimee looked surprised, Lucy clarified, "I know Camille quit at the last minute. I was actually present when she and Phoebe crossed swords on her way out."

Aimee compressed her lips. "Can't say that I miss her. Miss High and Mighty."

Lucy's lips quirked. "She did seem to have a bit of an attitude." Thinking maybe Aimee would have some useful input, Lucy pressed on. "I bet she was difficult to work with."

Aimee rolled her eyes. "That's an understatement. All she ever did was brag about how she almost had her own TV show."

Lucy cocked her head. "Really? Camille wasn't always a model?"

Aimee shook her head, patting her sleeve dry with a paper towel. "She was actually in the running to host the show that Vanna Verity wound up with, the one that skyrocketed her career. According to Camille, she was this close." Aimee snapped her fingers. She shrugged. "But they chose Vanna."

The rest of Aimee's words faded away as the implications of that statement hit Lucy. She nodded, pasting on a smile as the woman thanked her.

Aimee turned to leave, and Lucy jolted out of her reverie. "Aimee, I'd like to talk to Camille. Would you happen to know where she's staying?"

Aimee shook her head, looking puzzled. "Sorry, I don't. But I can ask around. I'll let you know if I find out."

Lucy murmured her thanks, absently saying goodbye. Her mind was clicking away, centered on one thing only.

Vanna and Camille had been rivals in the past.

or the rest of the afternoon, Lucy waited for Taylor to call her back. She was loath to disturb him again, but the information she'd just received could lead to the break in the case they'd been waiting for. She was itching to dig deeper into Camille's past, and resolved to do an internet search on the model when she got home.

Betsy and Aunt Tricia left just at closing time, while Hannah stuck around, helping Lucy finish inventory. They walked out to the parking lot together shortly before five-thirty, where Hannah was parked now, as well. Taylor had still not called her back, and Lucy was feeling annoyed.

"Hey, someone left a note on your windshield," Hannah observed, plucking it off and handing it to Lucy.

Lucy looked down at the folded note, surprised. *A note? Why hadn't the sender just called, or knocked on the bakery's door?*

She unfolded it, her eyes widening as she read the printed handwriting.

If you want to know who poisoned the cake, meet me at Fulbright Park at six pm. I'll be waiting on the bench by the fountain. Come alone.

Lucy gasped, her hand covering her mouth. *Who could have left this note? Did they really have information about the killer?*

Hannah frowned, seeing Lucy's reaction. "What? What is it?"

Lucy's mind spun. She had a sneaking suspicion that Aimee might have left the note. Maybe the young model was too intimidated to say anything while she was inside, but had second thoughts once she left.

Hannah suddenly snatched away the note, reading it with a puzzled expression.

"I don't get it. If this person knew who the murderer was, why not go to the police?"

Lucy bit her lip, then decided she must tell Hannah what she'd learned.

"I think it may be from Aimee, one of the models at Phoebe's shop. She came in today, and you wouldn't believe what she told me…"

She quickly filled Hannah in on all that had happened, including Phoebe's disclosure about the Crane's coming to see her, Dale and Camille's romance, and ended with the surprising news that Camille and Vanna were old rivals.

"I tried to talk to Taylor about it today, but there was some hubbub going on at the station, and he didn't have time to hear the details."

She turned a worried gaze on Hannah. "What do you think I should do? If I don't show up at the park, that might be the end of it. We'll never know. If I try to let Taylor in on it, you know he'll tell me to wait at home while he investigates. And if the note-writer sees anyone but me at the park, they might just leave."

Hannah was silent for a moment, musing. "Do you really think the note is from Aimee?"

Lucy scrutinized the paper. "It looks like a feminine hand to me. What do you think?"

Hannah squinted down at the writing and nodded her agreement, pondering.

"Maybe you should go. If you see anyone intimidating at the park, like a big, burly guy hanging around, you can just keep walking. It is a public place, after all."

She caught Lucy's eye, adding, "Why don't we decide on a time for you to call me and tell me you're OK? If I don't hear from you by then, I'll call Taylor."

Lucy nodded, relieved at the suggestion. "That sounds like a good plan." She consulted her watch. "If I don't call you by seven o'clock, then something went wrong."

"At which point I'll call in the cavalry," Hannah replied. She glanced at her watch. "You better get going."

They each got into their vehicles and parted ways, Lucy heading east, Hannah heading west.

———

JUST INSIDE THE PARK GATES, Lucy peered around a sycamore tree, locating the bench near the fountain. There was no one waiting. She took a quick look around. A few people were strolling down the paths, but she didn't see anyone who looked to be a threat.

She quickly made her way to the bench. As she reached it, she suddenly spotted an envelope taped to the wooden slats. Her name was scribbled on the front.

Another note? Maybe the sender had named the killer...

She withdrew the folded paper, her fingers trembling with excitement.

> **Meet me at the Dawson Hospital parking garage by six-thirty. Go to Level 3 and wait. I'll come to you.**

Lucy frowned at the message, disappointed. *This was starting to feel like a wild goose chase. Why were they playing these games?* She contemplated her next move, tempted to go home, but knew she would lie awake all night, wondering what she might have learned.

With a sigh, she walked briskly back to her car. It was a twenty-minute drive to the underground garage at Dawson Memorial Hospital. Hopefully, she wouldn't get caught in traffic.

Luck was on her side. Nineteen minutes later, Lucy passed through the garage's entrance and headed for Level 3. She glanced at her watch–eleven minutes to spare. She'd call Hannah and update her on the events just as soon as she found a parking spot.

Level 3 was mostly deserted, with only a few cars parked here and there. There was no one in sight at all. Lucy shut off the engine and pulled out her phone.

No signal.

Exasperated, she opened the door and emerged from her vehicle, holding her arm up, waving this way and that, searching for a few bars. *Nothing.*

She suddenly realized what the problem was. She was underground–of course there was no signal! Looking around at the deepening shadows, she began to get nervous. She really needed to let Hannah know where she was.

A quick check at her watch, and Lucy made her decision. She'd take the elevator to the top deck, which was open air, and send a quick text to Hannah. She'd be back down on Level 3 before six-thirty.

It was a good thing she'd arrived early, Lucy thought, locking her car and dashing to the elevator. She punched the up button and stood waiting, her thoughts drifting to Taylor. Somehow, she'd have to think of a way to tell him whatever she learned from this meeting, without him getting angry that she'd come alone. No easy task.

A sudden sharp pain pricked her skin on the back of her arm, startling her, and Lucy whirled around, wondering if she'd been stung by a wasp.

Terror seized her. A man wearing a black ski mask was looming over her, just inches away.

Lucy stepped back in shock and felt her world tip sideways. Her vision blurred, and she stumbled, opening her mouth to scream.

The sound never passed her lips.

Blackness closed in as Lucy fell to the pavement and passed out.

27

*M*uffled sounds slowly broke through Lucy's consciousness, and she opened her eyes, completely disoriented. She blinked, seeing nothing but darkness. Attempting to sit up, she discovered she could not leverage her arms. A chilling realization came over her: she was bound, hand and foot. Her pulse racing, she took stock, feeling a tightness across her mouth and realizing she was gagged as well. Her head felt funny. It was hard to focus.

Where was she?

Her heart pounded as fragments of memory came filtering through her mind. *She'd been meeting the sender of the note. She'd arrived at the parking garage and had gone over to the elevator.*

Her eyes opened wide as she recalled the sudden prick of pain on the back of her arm. *The masked figure behind her.*

She'd been jabbed by a needle. Drugged.

Panicking, Lucy attempted to move her feet to explore her boundaries, feeling her sneakers kick against a solid surface. It made a dull thudding sound. She rolled awkwardly to her right side; her face pressing into the rough carpet. It smelled like motor oil. A large, solid, curved object pressed uncomfortably against her shoulder.

A tire.

With horror, Lucy realized she was locked in the trunk of a car.

In a full-blown panic, she gasped for breath through her gag. *How long had she been in here? Was she running out of air?*

The muffled voices outside grew louder, and Lucy tried to quiet her breathing, listening.

Should she kick her feet to call for help? Or were her captors the ones she overheard talking?

It was a male and a female, and the male seemed to be on the defensive.

"I agreed when you said we had to cover our tracks, but I don't know... this seems pretty extreme. What if we get caught?"

The woman scoffed, a derisive sound. "Extreme? Do you want to go to jail? Because that's where you're headed if you don't listen to me."

A beat of silence, and then the woman's tone softened, murmuring something Lucy couldn't hear.

The man responded, sounding contrite. "Aww, please don't be that way. I *do* love you. Haven't I proved that? Haven't I done everything you've asked me to do? All I want is for us to get far away from here and live our lives together."

The woman replied, her voice soothing. "And we will, Dale. Just one more little loose end to take care of. And then it's just you and me."

With a shudder, Lucy realized the woman was Camille, and the loose end she was referring to was Lucy, herself. *What were she and Dale planning to do?*

The man mumbled unintelligibly, and Camille continued to placate him.

"It wasn't our fault. There was no way we could have known Vanna wouldn't eat that cake. I wish it hadn't worked out that way–she was the one who deserved to die."

Camille's tone turned bitter. "You don't know her like I do, Dale. She's a horrible, selfish person. Just think of how easy our lives would be if Vanna hadn't stolen that job away from me. I deserved that talk show spot, not her! I would have been a spectacular TV host. Don't you think so?"

Dale answered, his voice adoring. "You would have been the best TV host ever, darling. They surely wouldn't have canceled your show, like they did to her."

Camille murmured something softly, and then her voice became clearer. "It's a good thing you happened to bump into Aimee, or we never would have known someone was asking questions about me. It's time for us to get out of town, Dale."

Dale sighed. "I hate leaving Dad struggling like he is. Too bad Phoebe didn't just close up shop after what happened. That part of the plan definitely backfired on us."

Camille sounded stern. "We can't worry about that now. We've got one shot to get out of Ivy Creek before it all comes crashing down on us. I need you to do exactly what I tell you."

Dale mumbled his agreement.

"Good," Camille said. "I've made us a reservation at The Washington Hotel in Bardsley. I'll meet you there. First, you need to drive to that abandoned mall parking lot at the edge of Ivy Creek, near the bus station. I scoped it out–it will be perfect."

Lucy listened with growing fear, as Camille continued, her commanding tone allowing no room for argument.

"This is important, Dale. I'm counting on you. You can't be squeamish when it comes down to it."

Silence for a moment, and then Dale's voice replied woodenly. "I'll do it, but only to ensure our future together, Camille. You know I'd do anything to protect you."

"As I would for you, my love," Camille replied, her tone sweet.

Her next words sent an arrow of shock through Lucy, freezing her heart.

"Use the gas can in the back floorboards to torch the car. Take the bus to Bardsley and meet me at the hotel."

28

*hey were going to burn the car with her trapped in the trunk!*

Panic overwhelmed Lucy, and she shouted for help, her voice muffled through the gag. *Maybe someone else was near enough to hear.*

Camille rapped loudly on the trunk lid. "Quiet in there! Dale, you better get going."

Lucy continued to yell, kicking her feet for good measure. *They were already going to kill her. What did she have to lose?*

A moment later, the car started up, and Lucy was rolled from side to side as Dale navigated the parking garage. She figured she had one more chance to be heard when Dale paused at the gate. She prayed the gate booth would be staffed, not automated as it had been when she arrived.

Less than a minute later, the car stopped, and Lucy thrummed her feet against the side, yelling, but knowing her muffled shouts for help would be ineffectual. Whether or not the gate was operated by a real person was unknown, but she gave it the best shot she had. Once they were on the highway, she knew she wouldn't have another chance.

The tires crunched slowly over asphalt as they began rolling forward again, picking up momentum. Lucy's shoulders slumped in defeat.

What could she do? If Dale followed Camille's instructions, he wouldn't even open the trunk–she'd never have a chance to try to escape.

Tears pricked her eyes, and Lucy sobbed behind her gag, filled with despair. Even though she knew Hannah would be calling Taylor soon, no one would be looking for her on this side of town.

No one was coming to rescue her.

A surreal feeling suddenly settled over her, lending her strength. Maybe she was already doomed, but she wasn't going to go down without a fight.

Determinedly, Lucy worked at the bindings on her wrists, twisting this way and that, desperate to loosen them. Her skin grew raw, but she ignored the pain, feeling a small triumph as she managed to slip part of her left hand free.

Struggling earnestly, she pulled as hard as she could, and was rewarded by a sudden pop as she broke free of the bindings. She reached up immediately and ripped the gag from her mouth, taking a shuddering breath. There was no use screaming now; from the smooth and even feel of the tires on pavement, she guessed they were already on the highway.

Working quickly, Lucy twisted so she could reach her feet, and minutes later had them free as well. The next thing she did was check her pocket for her cell phone, but unsurprisingly, it had been confiscated.

Feeling around the trunk, she searched for a tire iron, but the trunk seemed to only contain herself and the spare tire. Next, she explored the trunk door's surface, trying to find an interior latch. She knew that all newer model cars were equipped with them, but her efforts proved fruitless.

Think, think... there had to be something she could do!

The taillights! If she could kick out the taillights... Lucy located the edge of the carpet and pulled hard, feeling it give. Two more good yanks and it came free, revealing a light patch in the darkness. She felt for the wiring and knew she'd found the taillights.

The cramped quarters made it difficult, but Lucy managed to swivel around so she had some leg room. She lined her toe up to the light patch and gave it a good kick.

Nothing happened.

Unwilling to give up, she kicked it again, and again, finally hearing something crack.

Yes! One more good kick and the plastic broke away. She could feel the open air flowing through!

Lucy bit her lip. She knew she was running out of time. Just waving her hand might go unnoticed. Quickly, she removed her sneaker and then her sock.

A white rag... a sign of distress.

Careful not to cut herself on the sharp edges, Lucy forced her hand through the opening and began to frantically wave the sock, praying there would be someone following closely enough behind them to see it.

The position she was forced to stay in was making her arm go numb. Setting her teeth, she ignored the pins and needles sensation. Doggedly, she continued to wave, desperate for someone to notice.

Suddenly, a police siren began to wail.

With renewed hope, Lucy continued to wave the sock. She felt the car surge forward as Dale gunned the engine, and she knew that a chase was underway.

The car rocked and swayed as the speed increased and Lucy was forced to huddle down, protecting her head from banging against the metal sides. She prayed they wouldn't wreck.

With a screech of tires, the car skidded and came to a stop. The momentum carried Lucy forward, slamming her into the spare tire.

Stunned, she lay there for a moment, trying to catch her breath. In a daze, she heard the driver's side door open, followed by pounding footsteps.

A voice yelled, "Freeze! Put your hands up!"

Lucy began to scream as loudly as she could. "Help me! I'm in the trunk! Help!"

She kicked her feet against the sides and pounded at the top. "Help!"

Suddenly, the trunk door lifted, the bright light of day temporarily blinding her. Lucy blinked, her eyes watering.

Officer Nelson from the Ivy Creek Police Force looked down at her, reaching in with gentle hands.

"Someone get Taylor on the radio!" he called over his shoulder, helping Lucy as she awkwardly emerged from the trunk, her knees feeling like rubber.

"We've found her."

29

"*A*untie, I'm fine, really," Lucy said, as Aunt Tricia fussed over her, laying a hand on Lucy's forehead. "The doctors gave me a clean bill of health."

Aunt Tricia looked dubious. "Less than forty-eight hours ago, you were unconscious in the trunk of a car. I'd say I have a right to fuss."

Lucy patted her aunt's hand. "Everything is fine now. I'm just a little banged up."

Though she didn't want to admit it to Aunt Tricia, Lucy had a good-sized lump on her head that was still aching from slamming into the spare tire when the car stopped suddenly.

The back door opened, and Taylor joined them outside on the patio.

"How's the patient, today?" he asked in a teasing tone, coming over to Lucy, who was stretched out on the chaise lounge. He dropped a kiss on the top of her head and Lucy winced.

He looked concerned. "Still tender?"

Lucy forced a bright smile. "I'm fine. Hey, Hannah and Miles are on their way over. He just got back. We're going to do our pet swap here."

"And not a moment too soon," Aunt Tricia commented. "Those cats are driving me crazy. Gigi has made it her mission to keep Spooky trapped under the bed."

A car door being shut sounded from the driveway, and soon they heard Hannah's voice. "Are you guys out back?"

Taylor answered, "We sure are!"

A moment later, Hannah came through the front gate, holding an empty cat carrier.

"Where's Miles?" Lucy asked.

Hannah set the carrier down, accepting a lemonade from Aunt Tricia with thanks. "He's walking Sampson. He'll be right back."

She settled into a chair at the bistro table, eyeing Lucy. "You look a bit pale. How are you feeling?"

"Fine," Lucy said with a quick smile. "Thanks to you! It's a good thing you called Taylor when I didn't check in. I thought I was a goner." She shuddered, reliving that awful feeling of helplessness, trapped in the trunk.

Hannah shook her head. "That was quick thinking Lucy, kicking out the taillight. Otherwise, the police never would have found you. Everyone was looking on the wrong side of town."

Aunt Tricia spoke up. "Did they find Camille, Taylor?"

Taylor nodded, his expression turning hard. "Thanks to the information Lucy was able to give us. Camille was waiting for Dale at The Washington Hotel in Bardsley."

He turned to Lucy, assuring her. "Both Dale and Camille have been charged with Debbie Ritner's murder, as well as attempted murder, conspiracy to commit murder, and kidnapping. They'll both be going away for a long time."

Lucy asked, "Did you find the poison that was used on the petit four?"

Aunt Tricia, setting down a platter of fried squash on the table, listened with interest as Taylor answered.

"We did when we searched the dumpster at Dale Crane's apartment complex. Apparently, it was the apricot glaze he'd poisoned, which he'd brushed on the cake prior to icing it. We found the remains of the glaze in a bottle and traced the source back to a purchase by Classic Fare."

Aunt Tricia shook her head. "I still can't believe Dale Crane would do such a thing! I've known that boy since he was knee-high!"

Lucy commented dryly, "Camille seemed to have robbed him of his senses, as love-struck as Dale was." She eyed the fried squash on the table, and Taylor noticed, immediately filling a small plate, and bringing it over.

"Thanks," Lucy said, teasing, "I could get used to being waited on."

Taylor sneaked a piece off the top of her plate and popped it into his mouth. He turned to Aunt Tricia, approvingly, "Hey, these are great!"

"Well, eat up," Aunt Tricia said. "I made a double batch."

"Hellooo, the backyard!" Miles's voice boomed out.

"Hello!" they all chorused, and a minute later, Miles came through the gate, being dragged forward by Sampson.

"Betsy and Joseph just got here," he informed them.

No one responded. They were all staring, open-mouthed, at Sampson.

"Why, Miles," Taylor said, putting a Southern drawl on his words. "Your dog is looking mighty pink…"

The ladies giggled, and Miles raised an eyebrow, turning to Hannah. "No one will notice, hmm?"

He looked down at Sampson fondly. "Yes, he is quite pink. As was observed by no less than five strangers on the sidewalk while we made our rounds."

"Pink's a nice color," Aunt Tricia assured him, sparking more laughter.

Betsy and Joseph joined them, entering the backyard as the laughter faded away.

"What's so funny?" she asked, then stopped short, staring at Sampson.

She covered her mouth with her hand, looking at Hannah.

"Tomato juice?" she whispered, and Hannah nodded.

"But it did the trick!" Hannah proclaimed. "At least he doesn't smell like a skunk."

"And that's a good thing," Joseph said, sitting down and piling a plate with fried squash. "Because if he was pink *and* stinky, that would be a bit hard to take."

He chewed and swallowed, exclaiming, "Hey, these are really good!" He looked at Betsy hopefully. "Can you make these at home?"

Betsy smiled, glancing at Aunt Tricia, who nodded. "I'll give you the recipe… and I've got a ton of squash left so you won't have to buy any."

"Maybe you should include that on the menu for your wedding reception," Lucy suggested. "She's not kidding when she says we have a ton of squash."

Betsy glanced at Joseph, their eyes communicating, before she turned to the rest of them.

"We've had a change of plans," she announced, prompting worried looks all around.

"You're not getting married?" Hannah asked incredulously, pausing in mid-bite.

"Oh, no, we are!" Betsy assured her hastily. She took a deep breath, looking around the table. "I hope none of you will be too disappointed…" She squeezed Joseph's hand before continuing.

"We've decided to elope."

The End

AUNT TRICIA'S FRIED SQUASH

INGREDIENTS:

- 2 large summer squash, washed and capped
- 2 cups of all-purpose flour
- 1 cup cornmeal (can substitute fine, dry breadcrumbs)
- 2 tsp. salt
- 1/4 tsp. black pepper
- 3 large eggs
- 2 1/4 cups milk
- 1 cup canola oil for frying (may need more)

PROCEDURE

Cut squash into 1/4" slices, set aside. In a large bowl, combine eggs and milk, whisking until blended. Set squash slices in to soak.

Pour enough oil into a large skillet to coat the bottom (no more than 1/2" is needed). Set on medium heat. The ideal temperature is between 350 and 375 F.

Combine flour, cornmeal, salt, and pepper. Spread on plate or shallow, wide container.

Shake excess liquid from squash slices, one at a time, and dredge in flour mixture, flipping to coat each side, and pressing down slightly.

Fry squash slices for 2–3 minutes per side, until golden brown. Add more oil, as needed.

Drain cooked slices on paper towels.

Serve while hot. Best if eaten immediately, but can be reheated in the oven (won't be as crispy)

Yield 24 to 36 slices, depending on the size of squash.

AFTERWORD

Thank you for reading *Poisoned Freebies at Phoebe's*. I really hope you enjoyed reading it as much as I had writing it!

If you have a minute, please consider leaving a review on Amazon or the retailer where you got it.

Many thanks in advance for your support!

TASTY EDIBLES, NASTY RUMBLINGS

CHAPTER 1 SNEAK PEEK

CHAPTER 1 SNEAK PEEK

"*H*ow many does that make?" Hannah asked Lucy. She rolled a rack loaded down with tins of unbaked cupcakes across Sweet Delights Bakery's floor, coming to a stop a few feet away.

Lucy stood at the five-shelf revolving oven, peeking through the barely cracked open door. Another five minutes, she judged, setting the timer. She turned to her number one employee and best friend, noting the weariness on Hannah's face.

They'd both come in extremely early that morning to fill the Morrison cupcake wedding order. Once they'd finished baking the order, they still had to fill, ice, and package five-hundred cupcakes by the end of the day, to be delivered to the country club first thing in the morning. It was days like this that had Lucy wondering if she should add seasonal kitchen help.

Lucy consulted her notepad. "We still have another eleven dozen to bake." She glanced at Hannah encouragingly. "That's nothing compared to what we've done."

Hannah sighed, wiping the sweat from her brow with her sleeve. "I think we should raise our prices."

Lucy nodded thoughtfully, tapping her pen. The price of supplies had gone up substantially in the past year. It would be the sensible thing to do.

The timer went off, and Lucy donned her oven mitts, opening the door as Hannah rolled an empty rack toward her. Lucy watched the revolving shelves, her hand on the stop switch.

Suddenly, the machinery groaned alarmingly, followed by a grinding noise. It came to a complete stop, with none of the shelves yet on level for unloading.

Dismayed, Lucy flicked the power switch off, then on, then off and on again.

"What happened?" Hannah asked, peering inside. Five shelves full of perfectly baked cupcakes sat in limbo, stuck where they could not be reached.

Lucy sighed, exasperated. She quickly shut off the heat and turned on the fan. With any luck, the cupcakes closest to the top could be salvaged–once the motor was fixed–but she knew the ones nearest to the heat source would be, quite literally, toast.

Leaving the door open to let out the heat, she turned to Hannah.

"Our day just got a whole lot longer."

———

An hour later, Lucy braced herself as the repairman, Simon Cox, stuck his head back out from the access panel. She'd known Simon for decades and trusted his expertise.

"Well, I've got good news and bad news," he said, wiping his hands on a rag.

"Good news, first, please," Lucy instructed, hoping the bad news was not too bad.

He nodded. "Good news is I can manually turn the shelves so you can get your product unloaded."

Lucy managed a small smile for his sake. That wasn't quite as good as she'd hoped for, as far as good news went. She'd already assumed he'd be able to do that.

"What's the bad news?" Hannah asked.

Simon compressed his lips, shaking his head. "You're going to have to buy a new oven. This one is so outdated now, there's no way I can get parts for it."

Lucy's heart sank, but she didn't doubt he was right. The oven, along with Sweet Delights Bakery itself, had been handed down from her parents, who tragically lost their lives in a car accident a few years ago. Almost all the equipment in the bakery was at least twenty, if not thirty, years old. Everything would have to be replaced eventually.

Resigned, Lucy nodded. She met Simon's eyes with trepidation.

"How much do you think a new oven in the same style would cost?"

Simon took out his phone and tapped it a few times before answering.

"A new one… you're looking at about twenty-eight thousand."

Lucy gulped. The bakery was doing well, but that was a huge investment.

"How about a used one?" She could feel Hannah's eyes on her as Simon consulted his phone.

"Well, it looks like there are several for sale in the state. If you went with a Blodgett, you could get one for about twelve grand."

Lucy sighed. That was still a lot of money. "Would it have a warranty?"

Simon nodded. "Yes, ma'am. I'd give it a good going-over for you to make sure it had parts that were easy to get in the future."

Lucy was silent for a moment, thinking. Obviously, they needed an oven. She knew that the five-shelf revolving ovens were pricier, but they worked out so well for her bakery.

She nodded. "I'll do it. I'll give you a call in the morning."

Simon saluted and turned back to their broken oven.

"Alright, let's get your cupcakes out of there."

Fifteen minutes later, they had salvaged all they could, and Simon packed up his tools and left. Hannah turned to Lucy.

"We need a plan. We now have fourteen dozen cupcakes to bake, plus two pie orders, as well as product to stock the store. Our little bread oven can only do so much."

Lucy nodded. "I'm going to call in a favor over at Bing's Grocery. They have two very large ovens. I'm sure they'll let us use one for a few hours."

They both heard the bell out front jangle as Lucy's aunt came in to start her shift at the counter.

"Reinforcements are here!" Aunt Tricia called out. A few moments later she poked her head into the kitchen. "How's the big order going?" She took one look at Lucy and Hannah's expressions and her eyes widened.

"What's wrong?"

"Let's all go sit out front for a minute," Lucy suggested. "Hannah and I need some coffee."

"And a chocolate croissant wouldn't hurt..." Hannah added.

Aunt Tricia listened sympathetically as Lucy relayed the events of the morning.

"Kind of bad timing," she commented. "Too bad it couldn't have lasted two weeks until the shop was closed for vacation. But you know, your mom and dad bought that oven more than twenty years ago, so I can't say I'm surprised."

She looked at Lucy over the top of her glasses. "If you need a little financial help..."

Lucy smiled her thanks but shook her head. "I can manage it, but thank you, Auntie."

She noticed the stack of mail her aunt had placed on the table between them and picked it up, flipping through it idly.

One envelope stood out from the others, the logo on the return address seeming oddly familiar. A line drawing of a cupcake with swirls above it forming a "C" and "B".

"What's that?" Hannah peered down at the letter, and her eyes widened with excitement.

"That's the logo for The Cupcake Bake-Off! Open it, Lucy!"

The Cupcake Bake-Off was a popular reality show, set in a different locale for each contest. Bakeries from across the country competed against each other for a large monetary prize.

Lucy's fingers trembled slightly as she opened the envelope, setting the typed letter down for all of them to read.

> *Dear Sweet Delights Bakery,*
>
> *You are hereby formally invited to participate in the Cupcake Bake-Off's 43rd contest.*
>
> *It will be held at the Howard Mansion, located on a private island off the coast of Georgia, during the third week of July.*
>
> *The contest will be taped for television viewing. Please RSVP at the number below.*
>
> *We wish you the best of luck!*

"Oh, my goodness," Aunt Tricia exclaimed. "I love that show! You're going to do it, aren't you, Lucy?"

Hannah scanned the letter. "How much is the prize?" Her eyes bulged as she pointed to the fine print. She looked up at Lucy with a grin, holding up her palm.

"Ten thousand dollars!"

Lucy grinned back, and high-fived her best friend, jubilant at their good fortune.

With a little luck and a lot of skill, they might have just found a way to afford their new oven.

———

Get your copy at all good retailers.

TASTY EDIBLES, NASTY RUMBLINGS

AN IVY CREEK COZY MYSTERY

RUTH BAKER

ALSO BY RUTH BAKER

The Ivy Creek Cozy Mystery Series

NEWSLETTER SIGNUP

Want **FREE** COPIES OF FUTURE **CLEANTALES** BOOKS, FIRST NOTIFICATION OF NEW RELEASES, CONTESTS AND GIVEAWAYS?

GO TO THE LINK BELOW TO SIGN UP TO THE NEWSLETTER!

https://cleantales.com/newsletter/

Made in the USA
Las Vegas, NV
21 February 2024

86046358R00108